P9-DGN-346

MILES FROM

ORDINARY

Also by Carol Lynch Williams

The Chosen One

MILES FROM ORDINARY

Carol Lynch Williams

ST. MARTIN'S GRIFFIN

NEW YORK

This is a work of fiction. All of the characters, organizations, and events portrayed in this novel are either products of the author's imagination or are used fictitiously.

MILES FROM ORDINARY. Copyright © 2011 by Carol Lynch Williams. All rights reserved. Printed in the United States of America. For information, address St. Martin's Press, 175 Fifth Avenue, New York, N.Y. 10010.

www.stmartins.com

ISBN 978-0-312-55512-2

First Edition: March 2011

10 9 8 7 6 5 4 3 2 1

For Aunt Linda.
I love and miss you.

MILES FROM

ORDINARY

I

There are mice.

Lots of mice. Running all over my room. Letting out crying sounds that grate on my ears. They crawl on my feet. My legs. I feel them on my arms. Soft things with toenails like blunt needles.

"Momma?" I say. She's dressed in a long nightgown. Her fingernails are sharp like the tops of just-opened cans. "We gotta get rid of the mice. We gotta call an exterminator." I hand her an old-fashioned phone.

"You're right, Lacey," Momma says. But instead, she cuts

at her face with her nails. Deep wounds open up, split wide, and blood, dark blood like ink, makes paths down her face to the floor. She cries.

"Stop that," I say. "Stop it now."

But Momma doesn't listen. Just cuts and cries.

I AWOKE with a start, my heart thudding in my neck. My whole body felt like I'd been dunked in an ice bath.

"Only a dream," I said to myself, then glanced at the clock: 3:46 A.M. I started to close my eyes. The wind nudged at the house. I could smell the magnolia tree.

Something moved in the corner.

"Hello?" I said, clutching my sheet to my chest. "Someone here?"

There was no answer.

The floor creaked near the closet.

"Hello?" I wanted to sit up in bed, but I couldn't quite move.

"Granddaddy?" My voice came out small. It felt like all the hair on my head was trying to get away from me.

"Lacey?"

Fear flashed a white streak behind my eyes. I gave a jump. "Granddaddy?"

"Lacey?"

Momma! It was Momma! Crying out a second time from her room. Her voice sad and scared and weepy. So the crying part of my dream was real. And maybe there was a mouse near the closet. A mouse coming from my dreams, alive and real? That was ridiculous. Of course that couldn't be.

"Are you okay?" I called to Momma. I kept my eyes toward the closet. Straining to see. Just darkness. No movement now.

The night breeze pushed into my room. The smell of the ocean. So peaceful. No more sounds from the closet. Good. Good. I took in a breath to push my fear away.

"Granddaddy," I said, hoping he wasn't close enough to hear me, "this is *my* room." A girl should at least have privacy in her bedroom. My heartbeat slowed.

"Lacey? I need you."

"Coming."

Man, was I tired. My eyes burned. But I threw my feet over the side of the bed. As soon as I touched the cool wood of the floor, fear surged in behind me. Run! I hurried toward my mother's room. It was like something chased me down the hall though I knew . . . *Did I?* . . . nothing was there.

A few more steps *Go, go!* and I made it. "What is it, Momma?" I leaned against the doorjamb. Her nightlight showed the pattern of flowers on the carpet.

"I'm scared." Her voice was shaky. Did she have a night-mare, too? "Granddaddy keeps bothering me. Has he been coming into your room? I've told him not to. To let you sleep because of tomorrow." Momma's voice wasn't even as loud as a whisper. I had to walk to the side of her bed to hear. I could see her slender form under the blankets. "And I told him *I* have to sleep too, because of you-know-what."

I nodded but Momma didn't look my way. Just gripped the sheet and blanket in her fingers and spoke like maybe I was glued to the ceiling.

"But he won't let me alone," Momma said. She glanced in my direction, then back again. "If you get in bed with me, Lacey, I think he'll stay outta here for a while."

Had he been to my room? For a moment I felt something behind me. Like someone watched. The feeling was muddy, heavy. Almost on my shoulder. Almost pushing me toward Momma. I refused to look back. Not that I could have seen much of anything. The darkness was fat, almost difficult, in the hall.

"Will you sleep here?"

"All right, Momma." Forcing myself not to hurry, *Quick, move it!*, I took my time. Granddaddy might be the boss of this house, but I wasn't going to let him know he scared me, too. I climbed in next to my mother and snuggled close. "Turn on your side and I'll scrooch up to your back."

4

"Okay, Lacey. Okay."

Momma was so thin I could feel her ribs. Could have counted them. I could smell her sweat, too. "You go on to sleep," I said. "If Granddaddy comes back in, I'll send him out."

Don't let him come in here. And then, *You know he won't.* And another, *He could.*

"Thank you, baby," Momma said. "You watch for him awhile. But wake me if he tries anything."

I yawned big. "I will." Here I was, all of fourteen years old, and I was crawling into bed with my momma.

You big scaredy cat, I thought. *Don't let him come in here. You know he won't. He can't. Not possible.*

With Momma so near, my fears faded some. My heart slowed. And at last I was asleep.

II

At 10:32 A.M., I moved away from Momma's sleeping body and eased myself outta bed. I sucked in at morning air, glad for daylight.

Today was to be a big occasion. Big for Momma *and* me. Both the Peace City Library and the Winn-Dixie grocery store had a nice surprise waiting for them. Us! *We* were headed their way to start our new jobs.

Please, please, please.

Into my room I went, walking on tiptoe, the hardwood

floor smooth under my feet. I glanced at my closet door, but it was closed tight.

"Just your old imagination, Lacey," I said, making my voice loud enough anyone listening in would hear me. "So get on with the day."

Before bed last night, I'd pulled out my clothes: a dark blue shirt that Momma said looks real nice with my eyes and a pair of tan shorts.

Now I was so excited, I felt a little sick. This was something I had wanted for a long time. I gazed at myself in the dresser mirror, pushing back my hair. My face looked okay, a little wrinkled on one side where the pillow had bunched up under my head. But I didn't appear too tired. I'd slept most of the night. This time.

"Peace City Library," I said, almost smiling. "I'm a-coming."

Jumbled-up nerves made me feel like I could take off running fast as the hummingbirds flit from hibiscus flower to hibiscus flower in our side yard. That's how excited I was about my new job. And jittery, too.

"Lacey," I said, leaning close to my image and running a brush through my long, heavy hair. "This summer is gonna be okay." I thought for a moment. Closing my eyes and letting my imagination spring out with the good crazies. "Maybe,"

I said in a whisper, "maybe I'll meet a friend." Opening my eyes, I wiggled my head at my reflection. "A girlfriend. And she can . . ." I hesitated then took in a breath ". . . she can spend the night. We can talk on the phone. Go to the mall maybe."

Nervousness and exhilaration ran out to the tips of my fingers. Anything could happen. Anything at all.

"Lacey," Momma called from her room. Her voice sounded weak. My stomach dropped a little. "Where are you?"

"Getting dressed. I'm coming," I said, but didn't move from in front of the mirror. I threw my nightshirt onto my bed, then slipped the shorts and top on. Flip-flops from under the bed *Don't look there* and I was ready to go.

"Is your granddaddy back?" Momma said.

I glanced at the closet. "No, he's not."

"Lacey, I need you to come talk to me." Her voice had gone whiny. Puny even. Still, her words were like Batman's Mr. Freeze. They stuck my feet to the floor. Cooled the blood in my veins. "I don't think I can go today."

"Oh yes you can," I said, low so she wouldn't hear me. There was no way. No way would I let this happen. I plopped the brush onto the bed, my hair half done.

"Unthaw, girl," I said. "Get going." In the mirror I could see two splotches of red on my cheeks. I turned fast and headed from my room toward Momma's. No arguments. Not now. I wanted out of here.

"You are in charge. This time, Lacey," I whispered, "*you* are in charge of the day and this job. Just . . ." I could only think of *be strong*. But *be strong* was like a sitcom. Be strong was what people said right before the end of the show and everything turned out good.

"Don't worry, Momma. I can help you get dressed."

Now that I was defrosted, I hurried, quick, into Momma's room. It was dark and stuffy, the nightlight throwing a small, yellow splash on a bit of the wall and the carpet, too. Those old flowers, plum-colored and different looking in the day. Not that you would even know that the sun waited outside if this was the only room you went into.

I flicked on the overhead light and then the lamp next to Momma's bed. Sat down next to her.

"Now Momma," I said. Something like desperation tried to claw at me, but I wouldn't let it. Stomped it flat. Pushed it away. "Remember how we practiced? Remember how we rode the bus downtown? Stopped you in at the Winn-Dixie and everything? Got the application. Filled it out. And they called you. You remember that?"

Momma looked at me, all dark-eyed, from the bed. Her body almost not there under the covers. She gripped her blanket and nodded.

"You can do this. And you yourself said we're running outta money."

"I know." She turned her head. "If only there was more. If only I hadn't spent it all. But you know I had to, Lacey." She looked me in the eye. "I *had* to."

"I know it," I said. "I know it."

"For you," Momma said. "I have to keep you safe, Lacey." Momma dragged a breath in. Sometimes the way she breathed sounded like work. Like it was all she could do. "A mother's duty is to take care of her only child."

"I know that," I said, "and you going downtown? Well, that is like you taking care of me."

She nodded a little. Looked away. Stared at the ceiling.

I reached out and took her hand. Her fingers were like little pencils. "The people at the Winn-Dixie are waiting for you. They want *you* to work for them. They want to pay *you*. You're gonna do just fine."

Now Momma stared in my direction. Her face smudged from not sleeping. Her eyes almost empty. But after a moment, she gave me a little smile. "I'll do it," she said. It almost sounded like there was an energy to her voice. "I'll do it. For you. For duty."

I grinned at her, relief coming to take the place of the almost clawing. "And I'll get breakfast going while you dress."

Momma sat up and I squeezed her tight in a hug. "I sure do love you," I said, my words like feathers.

"And I love you, baby girl." She patted my back, thumping her hands on me like I was a drum. "You are such a help."

Before she could change her mind, I ran from the room and down the stairs to the kitchen.

"Granddaddy," I said, grabbing the makings for pancakes. There wasn't anyone in the room but me, so I spoke to the air, throwing my voice where he would hear me if he was near. "Granddaddy, don't be bothering my mother today. She needs to be away from here."

Soon as I said those words, I remembered Aunt Linda. Right before she left she'd said almost that same thing to Momma. "Angela," Aunt Linda had said, "you need to get away from this house. You need to get free of those memories."

Momma had watched Aunt Linda, quiet. It had been like a showdown, something from TV. The two of them standing there, squaring off, face-to-face, eye-to-eye. If it had been a movie on television it would have been a western, and one of them would have drawn a gun. Shot the other right down. Dead in the street.

"It's not good for you to stay here." Aunt Linda had brushed back the hair that fell into her face. Her cheeks were colored bright pink. It's hard to stand up to Momma, but she had. Yes, she had.

And Momma had said, "This is *my* place. Don't you forget it. You hear me, Linda?" The words squeezed between her teeth. Shot into the air. Hit their target.

Momma had drawn the guns that day.

The thought of that fight still made me ache. And it was more than a year ago.

"Don't go there," I said, and started working on breakfast.

I had pancakes and eggs frying when Momma came down the stairs dressed for her first day of work. The window over the sink was cracked open an inch, and a morning breeze came in at us, freshening the room some, pushing pancake smell around. Momma's steps were slow and quiet— almost like a ghost. Outside green tree frogs called for rain.

"Close the window, Lacey." Momma flung her hand in a get-away gesture, like the motion could shut out the air, close the window itself. "You know they can't be opened. Not a good thing. Too much comes in through openings like that."

"Right," I said, and pushed the glass shut.

"New day for both of us," Momma said. "How do I look?" She turned in a little circle to model her Winn-Dixie apron. Her almost-black hair was swept up in a loose ponytail. I could see she was clean. *Good, good.*

"Whoo-eee!" I said. "Momma, there won't be a prettier checker in all the Winn-Dixies in the whole wide world."

She gazed at me, big-eyed. Her voice got all soft. "You mean it?"

"I do."

She was quiet a moment, leaning onto the counter. Thinking right over the top of my head. "Your granddaddy? I bet he'd be proud of me this morning. Yes, Daddy would be proud." She straightened tall, then glanced over her shoulder, toward the stairs that entered the kitchen. "Wouldn't you, Daddy?"

There was no answer.

"Absolutely he would," I said, throwing a quick look in the same direction. "Starting a new job and all." Outside, the sun fell through the trees and lit up the yard in splotches. I could see the bushes move with the wind. A squirrel sat at attention waiting for something.

Momma didn't say anything about my new job, just let out a sigh. A little grin came to her face. "I'll wait in the dining room," she said after a minute.

"And I'll serve you like you are a queen."

She cocked her head like a bird. "Your granddaddy used to say that to me and Linda all the time. All the time when we were girls just your age. Just ten and twelve. Called us his queens."

"Really?" Her words kinda gelled up my guts some. Had Granddaddy told me what to say in my sleep? Whispered it from the past? From out of the closet? *She's a queen. My queen.* Had he said that?

I shook myself free of the cold sensation. We had to get moving. I had to. "Now *I'm* saying it." My voice sounded thin. "I'll have breakfast to you in a minute and then we can go and wait for the bus."

Momma nodded and stepped light-footed into the dining room.

I let my breath out in a slow puff. Real careful I opened the window a little just so I could hear the call of the frogs. I moved the curtain some so it hid what I had done. Then I went back to cooking.

In a few minutes I took Momma's breakfast to her and set it on the dark wooden table. The room had a closed feeling—tight and hot. But the food made the air smell yummy.

"Mmm," Momma said. She looked up from the paper that spread in front of her.

"How'd you get that newspaper?" I asked. I set her plate down.

"Granddaddy gave it to me."

I peered around the room. "You didn't talk to him, did you?"

That's the last thing I needed. My grandfather poking his head in here at this time of day. Especially seeing the plans Momma and me had. He sure could mess things up. Sure could. He sure *had*.

Momma shook her head and with her fork picked at the pancakes. Her hands, I noticed, shook. I poured the maple syrup for her, watching the pat of butter that sat in the middle of the pancake flatten out and follow the syrup down onto the blue plate.

"Eat a lot," I said. "You wanna make sure you got enough energy to make it through the day. And eat those eggs. You need the protein."

The Gainesville Times covered half the table. I knew without looking that my mother had been reading the section that talks about catastrophes near and far. She seemed all right, though. Not too jumpy. Not ready to head back to bed. Just a little worry rimming her eyes. Shaking in her hands.

Please.

I settled into the chair next to her and started in on my food.

"Are you going to be fine without me?" she asked after a moment.

I looked up into her wide eyes. All of us, Momma and me and Aunt Linda and even Granddaddy have the same color eyes—dark like a troubled sky. Momma leaned toward me and smoothed my face with her hand. "You going to be able to do it?" Her hand was silky and cool. Gentle on my face. Tender.

I held still and let her pet me. I imagined her like somebody's momma from school. *She's like any other person,* I thought, though I knew it wasn't true at all.

"Will you be fine?" she asked again. She moved away, settling her hands on the table, like a bird resting.

"Yeah," I said. I nodded. Tried to swallow. If spit wouldn't go down, would food? "I'll be great." I cut at a pancake that was spread thick with soft butter. For a moment I remembered my aunt in here with us. All of us. An old memory. The way we threw back our heads to laugh. I couldn't have been more than five. All that laughter.

"What about you? Are you going to be okay? Should I go to work with you?" I asked. *Hope not. Hope not.*

"Me?" she said.

That one word came out so lean I could almost hear Momma's fear in it.

"Yes, you," I said, and fixed my eyes onto her face. All the sudden I wasn't so sure I should leave her. Would Momma be okay alone? She hadn't done any wandering since those first few weeks after Aunt Linda left. And I always found her. That was more than a year ago. But . . .

17

Momma swallowed a few times. Did swallowing trouble run in the family? She looked off over my head, like maybe somebody waited behind me. But there wasn't anyone there, I knew. I mean, I didn't feel anyone back there. Then she nodded, though her lips seemed thin and too pale. "Oh, I'll be fine. You know that. We always do good. Even with Linda gone."

No we don't.

"I know," I said.

Right at that moment it felt like fire ants ran a path through me. I love my momma like nothing else but I wanted out. I *needed* to be out. Before Granddaddy started pestering her again. Before he started pestering *me*.

Get us out, out, out.

I bent over my food then, and ate fast not looking at her. My stomach fwomped at the thought of getting on the bus and riding to the library. Of dropping Momma off for a couple of hours. Of us being separate. So nerve-racking! So exciting! I grinned.

"What's funny, Lacey?" Momma said. "Not much that's funny." Her voice was the color blue, cool and worried.

"I know, Momma." The pancake started to get heavy in my mouth. "I wasn't laughing about anything. Just thinking."

"You see that paper? The place where I circled the article

in crayon?" With a chewed-off fingernail she pointed at *The Gainesville Times*.

"'Tornado Sweeps Through Oklahoma,'" I read the headline out loud. "'Kills Sixteen.'"

"Two whole families were among the dead," she said. "Whole families." She raised her hand in the peace sign. There was syrup on her knuckle.

"Don't think about that," I said. I breathed deep the odor of maple, trying to ignore Momma's words. I could smell the newspaper. Could feel the wool of the carpet beneath my bare feet where I'd slipped the flip-flops off.

Eat, eat, eat. Don't think. Please don't worry.

"Coulda been here," Momma said, moving her head, her ponytail swinging. "Coulda been right here in Peace." She tapped at the table, then leaned at me. Her voice was low. "Coulda been *us*." Then her fingers went to work at the necklace she wears. I could hear the pendant making *zip, zip, zip* sounds on the chain.

"It *wasn't* here, though," I said, keeping my voice quiet. "It wasn't here. Don't think about it." I wanted to say, "Quit reading the paper. Put it away. Don't look for doom and gloom."

But Momma is doom and gloom. And Granddaddy doesn't help at all.

What would Aunt Linda do right now? I tried to re-member everything she would say to help Momma hang on to calm.

"Don't think about the ugly stuff, Angela." "Think happy thoughts. Don't let your mind wander. Focus on something sweet." "God is good. God is good."

Aunt Linda had a saying for every moment. Sayings for me, too.

Putting me to bed: "Sleep tight, Lacey-girl. Me and the stars are looking out for you."

First day of school: "You need anything, Lacey-girl, I'll drop everything and come right to that school and take care of whatever it is."

Early morning on a Saturday before she headed off to work, "The beach is calling our names, Lacey-girl. Wanna go for a run?"

For me, most everything Aunt Linda said was like a salve. Even as Momma got worse. And for my momma, Aunt Linda's words sometimes worked. Sometimes they didn't.

That just how it was.

Just how it is.

And I'd just as well try. Say something. If not, I'd be here another day. And another and another. The thought felt explosive in my head. "You gotta new day before you." My voice was a whisper.

Weak! What a weak thing to say!

Momma pointed at the headline. She worked at the pendant.

Then she glanced up at me.

"That's right," Momma said at last. "You are so right, Lacey. Yes, you are." She mashed her hands together then tried to smile. A bit of sadness seemed to drop off her. It rolled right into my heart. *I was so selfish. Why was I so selfish?* I squinched my eyes shut for a second.

"You know what I tell Daddy?" Momma said.

My eyes were still closed. I couldn't quite look at her. I shook my head no.

"I tell him that I got me the best baby girl in all of Peace. In all of Florida. In all the *land*."

I opened my eyes.

Momma stared right at me. "I tell him you are something else. *Something* else. And when he gets me to try and follow him, I say, 'Daddy, I got me a girl to look after.'" Momma reached out and ran her hand over my cheek, touching me with her trembling fingertips. "Yes, I do. I got me a child to take care of."

I pushed at the guilt that hurried through me.

Just let me be selfish for this one day. Just for one day.

And maybe the summer. Just let me have this summer at the library.

"Momma," I said. I took her hand. Squeezed her slim fingers. "Everything is going to be okay. We got each other."

"Yes we do, Lacey," Momma said. "You and me."

Keep her calm. Keep her calm. Keep me calm, too. This'll work.

"It really *is* going to be okay," she said. "Isn't it?"

"It really is. I promise."

She nodded like she believed my words. Then tilted toward me until our foreheads touched. I could smell her milky breath. Slowly, I rubbed her slim arm. Her skin felt so cool.

And I hoped. I hoped to goodness I had told Momma the truth.

III

The reason I even got me a summer-nonpaying-job-at-the-library is because of Aunt Linda. She used to work here—for lots of years. She knew everything there was to know about Dewey Decimal and his system. And even more about children's books. She ran that part of the library. She loved the Decimal system so much she had herself a little parakeet in a cage that sat up on the informational bookshelf where all the world could see him. His name was Mr. Dewey. When she quit her job and left, she took Mr. Dewey with her. The library hasn't been the same since. No chirping.

And no Aunt Linda.

"A helper at the library?" John had asked when I came in a week before school ended to find out about a job. "Any relative of Linda Mills is welcome here. But I need to interview you."

"Okay," I had said, trying hard not to smile. "Thank you. I mean, that's fair."

Shut up, mouth!

My heart thumped. Wanting to yelp for joy, but instead holding the happiness in, I waited for John. What kinda luck was this?

"You a hard worker?" he asked.

Believe you me, Momma's taught me that if she's taught me anything at all. "Yes, sir," I said.

"And are you willing to come in when we need you?"

If she says yes. If Granddaddy says yes.

"As long as the bus will get me here," I said. "We don't have a car."

John nodded. "I remember."

We haven't had a working car in a forever. When Aunt Linda left, she took hers. And right before that, Momma had the incident and now she's not allowed to drive, what with the way she ran us into a ditch one day when she was having a difficult time. Her words. If you ask me, the judge shouldn't have said "*no driver's license*" to her. It's hard to sob

24

and drive and see all at the same time. And we've needed a car, though I have made do on foot and by using public transportation.

"We can arrange your hours to work with the bus route," John said. He tapped his fingers together. And just like that I had a volunteer job at one of Aunt Linda's favorite places: the Peace City Library.

One of my favorite places, too.

Now, on the bus, sitting there beside Momma, I squeezed her hand again. Not because *I* needed it, though I *was* a little nervous. Momma was taking a big step. And I was real proud of her. Proud and hopeful at the same time.

Outside the sun beat down hot, making the green of passing trees bright. The sky was clear blue except for one bit of wispy cloud. It was cool on the bus. And loud. Every time the bus driver shifted gears or stopped to pick someone up, me and Momma jerked forward and backward in our seat. Momma had plugged her ears over the noise. And she wasn't looking at anyone, either. Just kept her face down, staring at her shoes or else the gum that was stuck to the floor.

"You're gonna do fine," I said to Momma, putting my mouth right next to her. Saying those words reassured me, too. *I* would do fine at the library. "You've run a cash register before and all the ringing-in stuff is done with a scanner nowadays."

"I know, I know," Momma said. I could feel her hand shaking. She bit at her lip. Peeked side-eyed at me.

"Remember how it's done?"

The day Momma filled out an application at the Winn-Dixie we had watched one cashier after another. Watched how each girl had scanned items, sometimes packing a small order herself. And Momma had been okay with it. Standing there kind of tall. Holding my hand till I thought my fingers might pop off one at a time.

"Not like the old days," Momma had said. "In the olden days we did all the work. Punched the numbers in by hand. Figured out the change. Counted it all out to the customer."

And I had said, "See, this will be a breeze for you. It's all automatic."

That watching gave her courage to let me fill out the paperwork for her. Gave her the courage to let me turn it in. Then to walk her to the man giving job interviews. I waited outside his office, my fingers crossed.

The bus brakes squealed as we stopped for someone to get off. "All you have to do," I said, squeezing her hands in mine, "is run the stuff over the reader thing and it'll ring in the price. And someone will be there to help you. You'll have a trainer. And a bagger too, for the first few days. They won't leave you alone."

"Still, it's scary," Momma said. Her head wobbled on her

neck, like maybe it might fall from its perch, roll up the aisle and then down the steps of the bus. "I only worked a year after your daddy left us. And then with Granddaddy's money I didn't have to work at all. Remember that?"

Yes, I did. We had never been rich. Never. But there had been enough. Until the spending.

"You remember Linda? She could do any kind of work. Any kind."

I looked away from Momma. Of course I remembered my aunt.

It was right then that I knew why I wanted this job.

Yes, there might be a friend. A girlfriend I could stay up all night talking to. But what I hoped, really hoped, was that my going down to the library would make Aunt Linda show up. Would make her come home.

Come back.

For a moment I saw us jogging along the beach together. The wind blew so hard that sand got in my mouth and I was still crunching on it at dinnertime.

There was me and her and Momma, before Aunt Linda left and Momma got too sick, having picnics in the park. All of us eating pulled pork sandwiches with a barbecue sauce invented by my momma's uncle Buddy over in Gainesville. There was the three of us, watching the Fourth of July fireworks out over the river, the night dark—the colors high and bright in the sky. And then just me and Aunt Linda, stacking books up ninety-nine high 'cause that's the checkout limit even if you are a librarian.

"Do you remember?" Momma said. "Do you?"

"Sure," I said. Something burned inside. "She helped us out."

"For a while," Momma said, her voice hard. "Selfish. She's just selfish. Leaving the way she did."

I bit my lip. Kept my mouth closed tight.

"She came at my invitation, not long after the accident. She stayed until she couldn't get another thing from us."

Not long after Granddaddy died, Aunt Linda had moved in with us. I was a baby. A tiny thing. Hair black and long and so straight it came all the way down to my eyes. I've seen the pictures. Me and Momma and Aunt Linda. Those two smiling and me with that long hair.

"Linda was always jealous," Momma told me once, "because your granddaddy and I looked so much the same. All that pretty dark hair. Like you, Lacey. And *she* looked like our momma who run off. Brown haired, a little chunky. Skin that tanned like that." A snap of the fingers.

"But we all have the same eyes," I had said. And Momma had looked away like I said a cuss word.

According to Momma, Granddaddy'd left all three of us with a tidy sum. Aunt Linda could afford to work at the library. Could paint like she wanted. Momma painting beside her early on. The two of them laughing. They both did a painting of the other one painting. Those are packed away in the attic now.

Then there was the change. Momma's mood shifting.

I still remember. I still remember sitting near her legs, wanting her to hold me. I was five, maybe six. The room dark. Her searching on the Internet. Looking for the bad things that were happening. Printing them off. Posting them. I still remember. Her too sick to touch me, pushing me away with her foot. Me edging closer under the desk. Momma too tired. Falling to the floor to sleep a few minutes at a time. Then Aunt Linda would come home and pick me up. Snuggle me close. Pet me. Make something for us to eat.

It wasn't long till Momma's part of the money kept her home watching the news and reading the paper, scanning for problems in the world. Keeping lists. Looking. Searching. And as night fell, her pacing, peering out the windows, locking things down tight. Not even a crack in the windows.

"I spent the money to get prepared," she'd tell me. "Spent it all to protect us. It's a mother's duty to take care of her only child. To make sure she's watched over."

"Yes, ma'am," I always said.

Now Momma said, "I'm not used to being around so

many people." Her voice was a whisper. She laid her head on my shoulder then and I patted the side of her face. "What if I get something wrong?" The bus hit a bump, bouncing us.

"You won't," I said. "I know it for sure. They've got that scanner. And people to pack the food in the bags for you. You know that. You've seen how they work. Everything is automatic. And you have the trainer."

"Sometimes I don't do so good," she said. Her voice was low and it pained me to hear it. To know she knew. How often did she notice she wasn't like other people?

"Shhh, shhh," I said. "They'll train you. You're gonna do great. I'm so proud of you."

And I was. So proud.

And relieved. And grateful too, for this chance to get out of the house. *Me, me, me.*

The very thought made me ache with guilt. But my want was greater than my feeling guilty. Maybe I'd see something left of Aunt Linda if I looked hard around the Peace City Library. She might be there. Waiting. Maybe she heard from John that I was starting a job there.

No, that was too much of a hope.

But. It. Was. *My.* Hope.

Maybe I would find a note from her. Written to me. Hidden in the shelves. A place where only I would know to look. A place only she would know where to hide it. I couldn't

30

quite take in a breath at the thought. Was it possible? What book would Aunt Linda choose to hide a note in? Something by A. E. Cannon? Or Claudia Mills? Maybe Betsy Byars. I knew Aunt Linda loved all those writers.

I squeezed my eyes shut for a second. There would be no note.

No note.

No Aunt Linda.

But maybe!

Just Momma. And me.

"I'm proud of you too, Lacey," Momma said. "I'm proud of you, too."

She kept still, all snuggled up next to me, small like a child. I felt her calm down. Could feel her take deep breaths, things she calls cleansing breaths that she saw someone do on TV to relax.

For a moment, something close to anger swelled inside. *I don't want to do this. I do not want to do this anymore.* But I pushed the thought away.

This was my job. My real job. Even more important than working at the library. More important than making breakfast. More important than school, even.

When Aunt Linda left, when Momma got worse, taking care of her became something I did. And I would keep caring for her, too. All I needed was a break. Just a short break.

I breathed with Momma, looking out the window, watching the dark trees sweep past. The old rickety houses on the outskirts of Peace. Condos. Then the beach—brilliant blue after the tight, closed-in woods.

This, I thought, *is gonna be okay.*

I imagined Momma keeping the job at the Winn-Dixie. I imagined her working her way up the food chain. Ha! *Food* chain. Maybe Momma would wind up getting the head cashier job.

And I would be the only volunteer in Peace City's history to be in charge of the whole children's library. John would call me aside and say, "Lacey, you have worked your way into a real paying job. Do you think you can work full time? Take your aunt Linda's place?"

"I've taken her place in lots of things," I would tell John. "Sure, I can do this."

But even with all the dreaming, inside there was a worry. I tried to keep it pushed down good with hope. And by ignoring the nagging feeling.

As we drove into town, stopping every few minutes to pick up new people, I tried to move my mind away from my mother. I had to think of something else. Something that made me feel better.

I looked around for someone to work with me in the library. Who looked like a real nice person? I must admit the bus did not carry anyone with potential. Lots of businessmen rode along, even more elderly people, women with their babies. Only a handful of guys near my age. One of them had too many tattoos for my taste. There were a bunch of girls in the very back of the bus, but they laughed way too loud to work in a library. Not one had book-checking-out promise.

"There's time," I said, low.

"Time," Momma said, in a singsong voice. "Time. Time, time, time."

But really there wasn't.

What I wanted, I decided sitting there on that hard blue seat, all I wanted, next to Aunt Linda, was a friend.

Anyone at all. That's what I wanted on my days out at the library. A friend. My cheeks turned pink at the thought of someone waiting for me at the library. A best friend for sleepovers and jogging on the beach, maybe, and even shopping for school clothes.

"I can tell what you're thinking," Momma said. Then she sang out, "Boys, boys, boys." She looked me in the eye. "I remember the boys." Her voice went soft and she stared out the window. "All those boys. Aunt Linda and me sneaking out at night. Stealing Grandaddy's car. Driving a carload of boys to the beach."

I knew the story. How Momma drove. How Aunt Linda

ran and tapped on windows, calling all the boys they were friends with to come on with them. Drive to the shore. Listen to the waves crash. Till the car was full of bodies and Momma was kissing her boyfriend while she drove. Swerving on the street. Almost running into a ditch from kissing and laughter, not from crying until she couldn't see.

Momma laughed now. Then her face grew tight. "You know Granddaddy wouldn't approve, Lacey. They will cause you grief. Men will cause you grief."

There was no use in explaining. "Yes, ma'am," I said. I thought of Granddaddy, so tall and lean, like in his picture, his eyes mad as a stormy sky. The way Momma and Aunt Linda had told me he was so quick to anger. And how he would mourn about their behavior for days. Keep them inside, watch so they couldn't sneak away, though Momma *could* sneak away, *did* sneak away.

" 'Oh, Daddy,' I would say. 'Angela and I are old enough to go to the dance. You don't need to worry.' " Aunt Linda's voice filled my head. This was just before she had left. Momma had been asleep and I had snuck into Aunt Linda's room to hear about her first crush.

I glanced away from Momma so I could keep my thoughts to myself. She wouldn't want me thinking of Aunt Linda. Aunt Linda was dead to her. That's what Momma said. *Dead and gone. Dead and gone.*

Gone!

I drew in a deep breath. This summer, I was sure, things would be different for me. If Momma and Aunt Linda could sneak away to be with friends, why, I could, too. The thought was like a fast-growing seed. Not *sneak away*. Just find someone to talk to. I'd start the journey to womanhood with a girl who was experiencing growing up, too. Not so far as Momma's gone. Neither of us would be like that. Not so unhappy. No, I prefer to stay this side of her unhappiness, which she says comes from her monthly periods.

"I been blue, Lacey, since the first day I started on the rag. I was thirteen and a half," she's told me time and again. I have the words memorized, say them right along with her. "It's hormones that does this to me," she says, spreading her hands out like a shelf holding sad information.

For a long time I thought hormones were snakelike things that somehow got into your gut and made you cry. Now I know they're more like parasites, sucking out people's happy feelings. They mess up Momma's days good when they're riding around in her body. I keep waiting for hormones to mess me up. But so far, I've been fine.

I glanced again at the girls at the back of the bus. One caught me looking and gave me the finger. I turned forward in my seat, my face burning.

Just past the cemetery the bus stopped again. And that's

when I saw him. Climbing up the steps. Showing his bus pass. Aaron Ririe from school. I looked away from him fast, then looked again. My face flamed.

"Boys, boys, boys," Momma sang under her breath.

I stared at my hands that were clasped so tight the knuckles had gone white. Aaron Ririe. I'd seen him in the halls. Even had an English class with him. And he's my neighbor. Lives just a couple of houses down the road from us. I looked up just as he passed Momma and me. Aaron raised his eyebrows to me as he clomped down the aisle toward a free seat in the back.

I wanted to melt away. He had seen me see him.

"He's so cute," I remembered Vickie Anderson saying about Aaron. It was one day toward the end of school. It had been hot outside and I had been waiting for the bus, standing alone, watching everyone.

"He sorta is," Alison Leavitt said. "A little. I guess."

"No, he *so* is." They had laughed.

I had looked at Aaron then and imagined myself coming up to everyone. Their circle would have opened for me. Vickie would have thrown an arm around my shoulder.

Then I would have said, without one bit of fear, I would have said to all those girls, "He *is* so cute. Such a hottie." I would have laughed right along with them.

But no one asked me how I felt. And I couldn't just walk

up and talk to them. So I stood on the outside, looking in, seeing them all collapse with laughter over Aaron. Finally, I had turned away.

The bus slowed down for the railroad tracks and I took a peek back at Aaron. He was talking with those girls.

"Who are you looking at?" Momma said.

I shook my head. "No one."

Aaron is a skateboarder. I've seen him on the road in front of our house, skating with his buddies sometimes, sometimes alone. Now I could see his board tucked right up underneath his arm. He looked straight at me, even with one girl leaning toward him, and nodded a hello. I tried to smile but my face wouldn't move and I had to look away again.

It took thirty-five minutes for us to get to the Winn-Dixie, and any time I wasn't talking to Momma, I glanced to the back of the bus. The girls got off at the mall, pulling at Aaron to make him follow. He grinned and shook his head. One threw a look at me and fake gagged. I gathered my courage and narrowed my eyes at her.

There! And ha! He's not going with you.

I looked at Aaron again as the bus doors closed. It was weird. And embarrassing. It was like I had to see him and I wasn't sure why. He was cute and all. But I never stare at guys. Not like the girls at school do. Even if I was in their group, I'm not sure I could stare at guys the way they do, laughing and giggling and talking behind their hands like it's a secret when really their voices are way loud.

But today, as we bounced toward the beach, the bus roaring along, I did look at Aaron. Maybe it was my library job that gave me courage to watch what he did.

And the thing is, every time I looked back, Aaron was staring at me. Twice he raised a hand in something like a wave. I swear my heart skipped a beat. Just like it says in books. I felt it miss, felt it thud.

"He is such a hottie," I said, my voice low.

"What?" Momma said. And then, "Boys, boys, boys. Oh Lacey, you know how Granddaddy feels about the boys. He's always watching, you know."

"Yes, I know Granddaddy's rules," I said. "I'll be careful."

"We're Fertile Myrtles," Momma said. "A boy can just take a peek at you, and you'll get pregnant. That's how fertile we are." She smiled like what she said was full of fact and like it wasn't the most horrifying thing a mother could say to her daughter.

"I'm not fertile, Momma," I said, my face flaming at the thought.

"You are! We are!" Momma let out a soft laugh. "Don't make eye contact with that boy." She nodded.

"What boy? I won't."

"You know what one," Momma said. She gestured with her chin. "The one back there."

I refused to see if Momma was talking about Aaron.

She whispered into the side of my face. "Granddaddy told me already you needed to watch out for that one." Momma gave me a smile that seemed so intense I was sure Granddaddy *had* warned her.

It was then that the grocery store came into view. I wanted to say, "What a relief. Take Granddaddy with you when you go," but I didn't. Instead, I leaned close to Momma, putting my arm around her shoulder. Touching her cheek with a finger.

"You ready?" I threw one last look at Aaron, who had changed seats, moving forward on the bus some. My face was bright red, tomato red, crayon red, red velvet, red like a fire, *no that's orange,* burning-hot red, I knew it. But I couldn't help the feeling I had. Aaron was cute. And on the bus. Right on this bus.

"Fertile," Momma whispered. Then she lifted her head. "Already here?" A look of panic swept over her face. "I've changed my mind." She gasped for air. Her arms tightened around me, squeezing out my breath.

"You can do it," I said, my heart picking up the pace a bit. I kept my voice low. "I know you can."

"I'm scared, Lacey." Her words were full of air. She looked me right in the eye and I saw that she was. For sure scared.

A good daughter would have done something different. Would have ridden all the way back home with her momma. A good daughter would have said, "Let's get on back to the house." But desperation grabbed at the back of my neck. For a moment I could only think of me. And getting out. Being free.

Then my heart went soft and I tried to talk Momma through her sadness.

"They're waiting for you, Momma." I spoke into the side of her face, my lips touching her skin. "And you can do this." I made myself say the words I didn't want to. I had to inhale big to do it. "Look, if you don't like your job, you don't ever have to go back."

"I don't?" Momma said. Her eyes searched my face, like she looked for lies.

"You don't," I said.

"And they're waiting," Momma said.

I nodded.

The bus pulled to a halt, one stop away from the Winn-Dixie. Momma took in a cleansing breath and let it out slow. "Well, I can't let them down. I've let plenty of people down in the past. Can't do that again." She touched her neck. "And if I don't like it, I can quit. You said so. And I bet Grand-daddy would agree."

"Now Momma," I said. "Don't you think of any of that. This is about money. Remember how worried you are about money? That's why you're here."

Momma's arms loosened a little. Then she pressed her dry lips to my cheek. Up close like this I could see tiny wrinkles near her eyes, near her lips. Her breath was shaky on my face.

"I remember," she said. She squeezed her eyes closed. "I can do this." Her fingers shook so that when she reached for her necklace I didn't think she'd catch hold of it. But she did. And as soon as she touched the small heart she said, "I can do this," again. Under her breath, "Daddy, *you* help me. I know you can. Daddy?" Her words were a prayer. A prayer to her dead father.

I glanced around the bus to see if maybe Granddaddy had materialized. I made eye contact with Aaron. He stared at Momma and me.

I ached seeing Momma like this. Guilt piled up inside. You know, for wanting her to go. For me wanting to be alone for a few hours. I almost took her arm and said, "Stay right here, Momma, we can figure something else out."

But what if Aunt Linda waited at the library?

What if she was there?

She might be.

Better to not miss that chance.

"You remember we're gonna meet at four-thirty? I'll pick you up just like we practiced. And if this isn't a good thing, why, we'll never do it again." Tears stung.

Momma kissed my forehead hard. "I remember, Lacey," she said. "I'll try to do good." She sounded like she was five years old. Again I felt guilt crawl through me. It knocked any embarrassment at seeing Aaron right out. But I didn't let that guilt stop my mother from going. I didn't say to her, "What do you say to us just going on out to the beach? Walking along the shore."

I *needed* her to go. Who needs their momma to go?

Bad girls do.

Don't think that!

Someone else pulled the bell, and a bunch of people stood to leave, including Momma.

"You look real nice," I said, touching her back. "Red's a good color for you."

Momma bent over and hugged me. I could smell lilac powder and shampoo.

"Four and a half hours," I said. "That's not so long."

"Right." She gave me a worn-out smile and wrung her hands, rocking with the bus movement. "Four and a half hours. That's not so long. I can do that. And I won't let anyone down, either. I won't. I won't."

"You are going to be the best they've ever had," I said. "People will remember you in the Winn-Dixie. They won't ever forget you."

Momma smiled, showing her small teeth.

The bus stopped with a loud gasp.

She made her way down the aisle, and every once in a while, turned back and waved. It was weird how I felt. Kinda teary, you know, like I might start bawling. When she got to the stairs Momma said in her thin voice, "I love you, Lacey Marie."

Somebody behind us let out a yelp of a laugh. A look of surprise crossed her face.

Who in the heck? Who would laugh at us?

"I love you too, Momma," I said, loud, making sure the whole bus heard me. I stood up so she could see me. "I love you, too."

At first I thought she might not move. But then she turned and headed down the stairs, the bus doors closing with a heavy air sound behind her. I watched as she walked across the black parking lot toward the strip mall where the Winn-Dixie was tucked in tight. She seemed so small. Like a good wind might take her away. Twice she looked back and waved. Then she was out of my sight.

IV

It was the tattooed guy. I know 'cause when I turned around to give the yelper a wicked look, he grinned at me. Aaron had moved into the seat behind him.

"I love you," Tattoo Guy said, his voice heavy with meanness.

"Mind your own business," I said, giving him the worst glare I could by stretching my face all out of shape. I stared him down hard, then looked away.

It made my heart pound, him laughing at Momma and me. Why, if Granddaddy could influence anyone *outside* our house the way he ran things *in* our house, I would have summoned him right then. But Granddaddy has a mind of his own—even dead. That's what Momma always says.

I looked at Tattoo Guy again. Who did he think he was anyway? And what had we done wrong? What was so bad about telling someone you loved them, if you did care? Even as I thought the words I knew there didn't need to be a reason.

"You lookit here, Lacey," Momma used to say as things were getting worse and worse. As Granddaddy was running things more and more. "The world is full of hate and meanness. It's full of lies and deceit. But we Millses, we treat people good, no matter what. You hear?"

How many times had someone at school said something ugly to me? Even before Momma was bad off. Before Aunt Linda drove away. Before I was alone watching out for Momma with Granddaddy peering close over her shoulder.

One thing goes wrong at school and they remember it forever.

Like Momma stopping by. That dirty housedress on. The lipstick. Her hair unbrushed.

Coming to my classroom door. Standing there, silencing even the teacher.

And me, looking up, seeing her. That her shoes don't

match. All us fourth graders, quiet like we're waiting for a surprise from the woman who looked scared even then. And me seeing it for the first time.

"Lacey?" Momma had said.

I didn't move. My pencil had become a tree trunk in my hand.

Mrs. Emery walked toward Momma. "Oh, Mrs. Mills." And her voice sounded normal. Just-like-always normal. "How are you?"

Momma didn't look at Mrs. Emery. She just took a step into the classroom and someone let out a giggle.

"Lacey, I can't find my medicine," Momma said.

Mrs. Emery gave me a nod I bet no one in the class even saw.

I stumbled making my way to my mother. Through a lake of embarrassment, I made my way to Momma where she grabbed me close, held me tight. And I went home with her to find her pills that were sitting right there in the medicine cabinet.

No one forgot that.

Sometimes still someone will say something about that day. Vickie Anderson might. I hear them. Behind my back most of the time. Once in a while to my face.

Later, Momma got sicker. Later, she wandered the streets

at night. Turning up on people's front porches. Once walking in on another family's dinner, sitting herself down at their dining room table.

How many times had I come in from the school bus crying? How many times had I said to Aunt Linda, "How do they even know?"

"Know what, Lacey-girl?" Aunt Linda smoothed back my hair. Set my math and history books aside on the antique bookcase we used as a catchall in the foyer.

"Momma," I said, my voice a whisper. "They pester me about Momma all the time. They've seen her just that once in class. How do they know?"

And Aunt Linda, her face unhappy, had said, "It sounds like their parents have been talking."

Lots of the people in the old part of Peace, lots of them went to school together themselves. They married each other, lots of them. They stayed here. These people knew Momma before. Before she was sick. Before Granddaddy died. Before I was born.

"Don't they know her?"

Aunt Linda nodded. "The way she was? Yes. Maybe they remember her a little quirky. But seeing her wandering, seeing her so changed," Aunt Linda let out a sigh that could have moved the leaves of an old oak, "it might scare them. Angela isn't who she used to be."

"She wouldn't hurt anyone," I said to Aunt Linda. I knew my momma. Afraid, yes. Worried, yes. But at this time she still sat on my bed, holding my foot till I went to sleep. She still read to me, laughing at the funny parts of books Aunt Linda brought home. Crying when she read aloud something sad.

That day I asked Aunt Linda the question that sat perched in my brain, staring over all my thoughts.

"Was Momma always different?"

My aunt had looked away. Then she shook her head. "Not really," she said, after a long moment. "Fun. Silly sometimes." She drew in a big breath of air. "I remember once we were just like fifteen and seventeen? And she dared me to sneak away with her in the middle of the night."

"You're kidding?"

Aunt Linda nodded. "She dressed up fine, put on these high heels she'd bought from the five-and-dime and hidden from Daddy, then we snuck right out her window—you know from your room?—and walked to where this party was going on. Like a mile or two." Aunt Linda let out a laugh at her memory. "She didn't even take off those high heels. Just marched right over to Bobby Valentine's house. I was so scared Daddy would know we were missing. That he'd get in his truck and follow us. But he didn't even find out. And your momma . . ." Aunt Linda paused and grinned.

"What?" I said.

"Your momma got to that party and danced on a coffee table for all to see. She kept those shoes on and danced!"

My momma had done that? No way!

"I was so embarrassed," Aunt Linda said. "But, also, I was so proud of her. There was no one like your mother, Lacey. No one. And man, did we ever have a good time."

"Then why?" My hands were a tight ball in my lap.

"She's always been a little sad," Aunt Linda said. "Even then." She shook her head. "Momma's leaving and not taking us was tough on both of us. But harder on your momma. She became the mother, sort of. Doing what mothers do, cooking, cleaning." Aunt Linda paused. "And your grandfather did strange things sometimes."

I hadn't asked Aunt Linda what. I already knew a bit of that.

Maybe Momma was right, I thought as the bus rocked and swayed toward the library. Maybe staying away from the world was good. If people acted like the Tattoo Guy all the time why be a part of that?

I rested my head on the seat back and wondered at Momma. I said a prayer in my heart for her. That she would be okay. That she would make it. That she would love her job. That she would be her quirky self once again, dancing on a coffee table in new high-heel shoes, at least for me to witness.

That who she was would step from the past, like a ghost splitting the skin of a being, and she would be okay again.

Maybe, I thought, maybe she would like this job so much she'd ask for extra hours. Maybe this job would fix her up.

It was a nice thought. Comfortable.

It surprised me good when Aaron plopped down in the seat behind me.

I popped my head up, turned, and glared at him.

"We don't live too far from each other," he said, like he couldn't see my squint-eyed angry look. He smiled full on, his face so bright I almost had to glance away. "We go to the same school, too. Do you remember me? We were in English together last year. With Mr. Humphrey. I talked to you then? Asked you about homework and stuff?" Aaron slung his hair to the side with a jerk of his head. It slid back into his eyes.

I needed to stay angry. Not let them hurt me. I peered over my shoulder at him. Why, I would hate him too, just for sitting near Tattoo Guy. I regretted all the looks we had shared during the bus ride. But he was so cute. So *hot*. Such a *hottie*. Aaron's long sandy blond hair hung loose, dropping to his shoulders. It curled some at the bottom.

"I was in Mr. Averett's homeroom? Aaron Ririe?" He leaned over the seat a little, his tanned arms near my neck. I moved to face him better.

"So?" I said. There was a nasty feeling crawling around inside me like a worm. It was all Tattoo Guy's fault.

And Momma's.

No! Not Momma's. *Tattoo Guy's.*

Aaron didn't even flinch at my rudeness. "Do you remember me? I said hi to you a few times? And talked to you about *Great Expectations*?" He paused. Shook his head, then said, "I hated reading that book."

I raised my eyebrows. "I love that book," I said. "And I remember you." All the girls chattering about him and his skater friends and Jace Isom. I felt my face warm up thinking about Jace. That group was hard to forget. In class Aaron spoke so low you could almost not hear him. He smiled a lot.

The whole ride today he had seemed nice.

Until the Tattoo Guy called out.

"Cool." He grinned, showing white teeth that were a little crooked. "I live across the street from you? Down a few houses?"

Why was everything he said a question?

He slung his hair from his eyes again. "You know, in that newer subdivision?"

Me and Momma, we live in an old place. Our house is so ancient that when the wind blows Momma says it's spirits running through looking for peace. "Granddaddy," she says on bad nights, "I hear Granddaddy searching." When there's a storm, and the wind shakes the walls like a thousand hands I'm not so sure I don't hear Granddaddy, too.

"I skate in front of your place?" Aaron's face turned red like he was running out of energy. His voice went soft the way butter gets when you leave it out of the fridge too long. Like he was embarrassed for something he'd done. Or my not saying anything. Well, good!

Good?

A horrible thought came into my head. Maybe, maybe, he had heard Momma. Had seen her during one of her frightened evenings. Had she climbed his front porch? Knocked on his front door? Told people to beware the evil that was coming to destroy the world? The thought horrified me. The thought sealed my lips even tighter.

Please God, don't let Momma have paid his family a visit.

"Okay then," Aaron said, and shifted like he might get up.

Speak, Lacey, I thought. *Now. Or he'll leave.*

I cleared my throat. "Yeah," I said. My voice sounded like I needed a sip of water. "I know about where you live. And I've seen you, too. You know." I pointed to his skateboard. "With that."

When I realized that Aaron Ririe's family had moved into the new subdivision a few years back, I'd taken to watching the street in the late afternoons. He sometimes skated in front of my house, most of the time with his guy friends.

There were five or six of them. Jace Isom was there, too. They laughed loud, skated hard.

Sometimes.

Sometimes at night, when the house settled in and before Momma called for me, I tried on the idea of me skating with that Jace Isom. In my imaginations he would say, "Good job, Lacey. You're a natural." He would touch my hand the way boys touched girls in school. His words would be kind. Not the things he had said.

Again, the memory of my dreams caused my face to burn. I looked away from Aaron. We were both quiet a moment. Did he know what Jace had said?

"Do you know Jace Isom?" Aaron said.

Could he read my mind? Like Momma? Like Grand-daddy?

"He was in your homeroom, I think. And some other class?"

"I know him," I said. Had the air-conditioning quit working on the bus? Why, it felt like I had stuck my head in an oven under the broiler. Knowing Jace Isom was a kinda truth. Kinda because Jace and I *were* in the same classes just a week ago when school let out, but I'd never really talked to him. Or anyone in our eighth-grade class for that matter.

But you thought about him. And you looked at him. He called you "Freak."

You are a freak!

I'm not.

You are!

The bus let out a sigh and I stared at the huge tinted window, not seeing anything outside. In the reflection of the glass I seemed like a ghost, a freakin' ghost.

I shook my head. Don't think of that, Lacey. Don't think of Jace or Tattoo Guy or any boy for that matter.

"My stop's coming up," I said. Ahead the library squatted like a coquina-rock bug, half of it on land, the other half perched out over the Peace River on huge concrete legs that had been driven into the shallow water. I could smell the ocean now. I pulled the buzzer. The bell sounded.

"No way," Aaron said. His face broke out in a wide grin. "Mine, too."

"No it isn't." My face went from hot to cold with his words. He was making fun of me. Like the other kids in school. He must know about Momma. It seemed at that moment, sitting on the plastic seat of the bus, *everyone* knew about Momma. Well, I wasn't going to take it! I wouldn't!

I glared right in Aaron's face, something I would have *never* done in school. *Never.* In school, after Jace, I kept my stares to myself, where no one would notice.

"I swear this is where I get off," Aaron said, raising his

hands like the truth might be on his palms. He let out a little laugh. His voice stayed soft. "Skate park." He tapped his board to prove what he said was true. I saw his arm was road-rashed near the elbow. "I go almost every day. And I skate at home. But you know that already."

I rocked forward with the movement of the bus. I gazed at Aaron good. His eyes were the color of melted Rolos—a smooth chocolate with mixed-in gold. Maybe he wasn't like Jace. Or the others. Maybe . . .

He is. You know he is. They are friends.

Maybe not. I mean, I knew they were friends. But maybe he was different. I could try to trust him. I could try. Momma was trying by getting a job. I could try by giving Aaron a chance.

He stood. "Where are you going?"

Answer, mouth. "To work." A birdlike feeling fluttered in my stomach when I said those words. I relaxed a little. "I'm going to work in the library."

"Oh yeah? You have a job there?" Aaron said. "Cool."

"Yes. Cool." It was cool. I pulled up my backpack and scooted around a little to loosen my legs from the seat. They were stuck from the humidity and heat, even though air-conditioning filled the bus with a soft hum. I was embarrassed to leave two wet prints shaped like triangles behind. Maybe Aaron wouldn't notice.

The bus slowed with a squeal. I stood. If *I* didn't look back, *he* might not see my sweat. There was so much to worry about. So much. No wonder Momma couldn't handle this. Too many things. Lots of them icky. Aaron came up close behind me, bumping into me as the bus braked.

"I love you," the Tattoo Guy said, his voice riding up to where I stood.

It felt like my eyeballs bulged from my head, like a cartoon character's.

"Shut the eff up," Aaron said. Only he said the *real* swear, the *real* word. Now my eyes did bulge.

Wicked. He's wicked.

"Just ignore him," Aaron said. "What's your name?" He stood close to me. Close enough that I could feel the rough top of his board on my arm.

I didn't answer. As soon as the doors opened I hurried from the bus, stepping into heavy air that smelled of salt and water. The sun felt good on my face. I closed my eyes and people stepped off the bus around me.

If today was going to be a good day, a different day, then I had to make it that way, bad words, Tattoo Guys and all. Opening my eyes, I squinted in the light.

"Lacey," I said.

"Huh?"

"My name. It's Lacey."

"Yeah," he said. "I know."

I looked toward the library almost glowing in the Florida heat.

He knows, he knows! He's one of them.

"Then why did you ask?"

"So you'd tell me."

"What?" I tossed my hair over my shoulder. It fell like a heated blanket on my back. "Why would you do that?"

He shrugged, looked down at the sidewalk, then back at me. "Just wanted a reason to say something. Asking your name seemed good enough."

"Even though you knew it?"

He leaned toward me some. I made sure not to step away, not to flinch. "It was an excuse, Lacey," he said. "An excuse to talk to you."

"Oh." He *wanted* to talk to me? *Me?* The bus roared away, leaving behind its dirty smell. I stood there staring at Aaron. My heart thumped.

The sun made the air seem full of foil-reflecting brightness. I needed to get inside. I needed to start working. Help people. Work long enough to stop my worry of Momma. Maybe even relive this conversation with Aaron who seemed nice. Nice to me.

Maybe, I thought, maybe summer was going to mean

lots of wonderful things. A job, Momma working, and a friend of my own. Maybe Aaron didn't know a thing about us. Maybe he had missed it all.

"I better go," I said after soaking in the sun a moment or two more. "I don't want to be late."

Aaron moved up next to me. "How long are you working, Lacey?"

Behind us traffic moved toward the beach. A horn blared. A salty breeze blew in from the water. I could hear the cry of seagulls.

Answer, Lacey, answer!

"About four hours," I said. I backed toward the steps of the library. "I better go in."

Aaron stood still, watching me. "Okay, bye," he said. He didn't move.

"I'll see you later," I said.

"Sounds good." Still, he didn't move.

I stopped on the library steps.

"See ya," he said. Then he spun around and walked off down MacClenny toward the big tree park, where ancient magnolias had grown so huge the limbs had to be propped up with metal poles.

I let out a huge breath of air. A good thing! This was a good thing! I felt—powerful. I marched myself (with power) toward the library where I'd dust videos (with power) and help old ladies reach novels off the top shelves (with power) and clean candy off the covers of books (with even more power and maybe some elbow grease). At least that's what I thought I'd be doing. Whatever my job might be, my day would only get better.

I'd gone up four steps and was almost inside when I heard Aaron call, "Hey, Lacey? I'll ride back with you. On the bus."

I shielded my eyes to look at him, not sure what to say. "Okay."

"Okay." Aaron grinned at me.

I grinned, too. Aaron waved a little. Then threw his board onto the ground, ran after it, jumped on and rode away. The wheels made *click-click* sounds on the sidewalk.

For several moments, again, I stood in the heat of the day. I faced the sun. Today was a wonderful day. A terrific day. It *was* going to be different.

"You are gonna make it, Lacey," I said.

I climbed the rest of the stairs, my face feeling strange for all the smiling I'd done in the last few minutes. I stopped long enough to pet the huge marble lion that pawed at air. Then I went into the library.

V

That first whiff of the library sent me straight back to Aunt Linda. I almost expected her to come from behind a stack of books like that had been her hiding place for the last year. Almost expected her to say, "I was just kidding when I left, Lacey." Or, "I've been here all along. Right here. Hiding!"

I glanced around, just in case. I could see the ocean from here, out to the east. Saw the adult section of the library, the computers where several teenagers sat, and the tables where an older man read the newspaper.

Was he looking at the tornado article? Was he wondering how a whole family could die at the same time? Or was he reading something others would think normal? Something *not* scary. *Not* sad.

One last glance told me Aunt Linda wasn't here. That book smell made me miss her something awful. For the second time in fifteen minutes, tears stung my eyes.

I'm gonna cry, I thought with surprise. I squeezed my hands tight. Pressed my fists into my hip bones. *I'm gonna cry.*

"No you aren't," I whispered. "Oh, no you are not." I don't cry anymore, not even when I get hurt. It doesn't help anything. Just plugs your nose and makes your face blotchy. Believe you me, I've seen that look too many times on Momma's face to want it on my own. That's why I was surprised at my own almost blubbering. Instead of boobing, though, I took in another breath, pulling in that Aunt Linda smell, and walked to where John sat behind the counter.

"Lacey," he said. He smiled like he was happy to see me. "Glad you could make it. And on time. Just like Linda."

I nodded. Again tears threatened. I hadn't realized I missed her so much.

This stinking library. It wasn't a Band-Aid. It was a jab at an old wound. The picking of a deep scab. I heard Aunt Linda's voice in my head: "Baby, you can sit on my lap as long as your feet don't touch the floor." She told me that any time she read to me. I always made sure after I hit a growth spurt to tuck my knees up high so not even one of my toes touched the ground.

"You ready to work?" John said, he clapped his hands together with an airy *pop*.

"Ready," I said. I could do this. "What are my duties?"

John gave me a funny look then said, "Your duties. Hmmm. First thing, empty those carts. You sure you know the Dewey decimal system?"

"Since I could walk." Okay, an exaggeration, but not by much. Momma knows it too, thanks to Aunt Linda. Once, a long time ago, I helped Aunt Linda arrange all the books on her bedroom shelves just like Dewey Decimal would have done it. I couldn't have been more than seven.

"I thought you'd want to do the kids' section. So have at it."

"All right."

Three pale green carts waited. I grasped the cool metal handle of one and pulled it across the speckled carpet. The wheels squeaked out *eep, eep, eep* sounds. Toward the children's section. Toward Aunt Linda's old job. My heart thumped with excitement. The tears were gone, dried away.

In my head I heard Aunt Linda's voice, soft like a night breeze. "Lacey-girl, books take you anywhere. Any place you want to go. You remember that always."

And I have.

From the moment I watched Aunt Linda drive away in that old gold-colored Mazda of hers, I've been reading. When I can, I mean. When Momma doesn't need me. Miss Docker, our school librarian, said I was her very best customer, and I bet I was.

Now, I'd be working where my aunt had worked. Surrounded by books of all kinds. As long as Momma allowed it. As long as Momma could work at the Winn-Dixie. As long as Momma was okay.

VI

Being in the library brought memories of Aunt Linda back heavy. There I was pulling that old cart around and it was like Aunt Linda sat on the big rocker in the corner. I mean, I didn't really see her, like Momma sometimes sees Granddaddy, who's been dead since my birth. It was like I *remembered* her being here.

Aunt Linda with kids around her at story time. Even the big kids would kneel at her feet as she read. Dressed up in a pioneer dress if she read something from the Little House series. Or with long fake red nails if she read *Holes* aloud.

Or with a fat mane of golden mop hair when she read *The Lion, the Witch, and the Wardrobe.*

I have a secret. It's one that turns me cold, just at the remembering. It's one that splits at my heart if I give it too much thought.

I know why Aunt Linda left.

Momma has no idea I listened in on their fights. Can't imagine what she would say if she knew.

But I did. I listened in every night, sometimes with the feeling of Granddaddy looking over my shoulder listening, too. And I knew. Just like that I realized Momma wasn't gonna change and Aunt Linda wasn't gonna budge, though really, in a way she did. In the end, I mean. She left, after all.

"Angela, you know I can't do this much longer." Those were Aunt Linda's words to Momma. In my memory I sat crouched in the hall, like a kid in the movies who listens in on people. "I've tried to get you help. I've taken you to the hospital when you'd let me. I've tried to keep you on your meds, but you just won't take them. I can't watch you kill yourself this slow way even a day more."

When I heard Aunt Linda say that, I tell you, the blood grew thick in my veins. Was Momma . . . I couldn't even think the word. But I sure could hear them fight about it.

And Momma's reply: "Killing myself? Don't you say that to me. You hear? Don't you say I am killing myself, ever. You don't know who I am."

Peeking over the rail in the hall upstairs, I saw Aunt Linda lean toward Momma. My mother's face was angry red. Her teeth clenched. Her whole self seemed to tremble.

"I know who you *used* to be, Angela. You change more and more every day."

Momma's hand went up in the air. Not like she was gonna hit her younger sister or anything. But to point in her face, though, truth be told, the pointing was just a weak jab. "And who was that?"

"Someone who was alive," Aunt Linda said. Her voice was so quiet I had to move forward to hear it. "You went outside—don't you remember your garden? You haven't been out there in years. You used to laugh." Now Aunt Linda lifted her own finger. "You spent real time with your daughter— held her, hugged her, *listened* to her. You weren't the walking dead."

"Don't you dare," Momma said. "Don't you dare bring Lacey into this."

Why? I wondered that night. And I've wondered it since. Why didn't I matter enough to be in that conversation?

The argument went on a while longer. Then the awful

part. The worst part of all. Both of them screaming. Yelling. And then Momma hollering. Those terrible words. Her voice screeching.

"Linda, I want you out. I want you out of my house."

"What?" Aunt Linda had said. She looked like Momma had slapped her a good one in the face. "You can't make me leave my home. I was born here. I grew up here."

"I can," Momma said. "And I will. This is *my* place. Daddy left it to *me*. And I can choose who stays and who goes. And you"—Momma jabbed again at my aunt—"you are going. Get out."

Those last two words were a scream. High and loud. It hurt my ears.

And before I knew it, I was hollering in the mix. Up above, looking down on them, yelling, too. Then running down to them both. That old T-shirt I slept in not even covering my underwear. I missed the bottom two stairs. Fell to my knees, skinning one so that it stung when I took a bath the next day.

"No! Don't make her go." Momma and my aunt looked up, surprised. I could see the tears on Aunt Linda's face. Could feel my own. Fear was thick, scaring me. I had to do something. Save Aunt Linda, and in the process, I knew I'd be saving myself. "Momma, please don't."

Momma's face went all confused, like she was trying to

make decisions right at that second. You could see it all there. By the way she looked at me and then Aunt Linda. All of us crying together. Standing in the half-dark living room. The night pushing in on us.

Momma didn't say anything more than, "You heard what I said, Linda." Her voice was near the floor. Then she went to her room, slamming the door shut.

For a moment Aunt Linda didn't even move. Then her shoulders slumped. Her head bowed. She went to Momma's door and called through to her, telling Momma that she didn't want to leave. She didn't want to leave me. I stood there next to Aunt Linda so close I could smell her perfume. So close, her arm brushed on mine as we knocked on Momma's door. I stood there, calling. Calling in, "Momma? Momma?"

Aunt Linda turned. She took hold of my arms in a tight grip and got right in my face. Her breath smelled like bacon. "I'll take care of you, Lacey," she said. "I swear it. I'll do what I can to get you with me."

"What?"

"I'll make sure you're safe."

I whispered, "I can't leave Momma. You stay here."

Aunt Linda was crying. Not making a sound but the tears ran outta her eyes and fell right off her chin. "If she'll let me stay." She leaned her forehead on mine. "But if she won't,

Lacey, I'll talk to the police. And to a judge. To whomever I have to talk to. And I'll get you with me."

"I can't leave Momma," I said again. "Who will take care of her?"

Aunt Linda pulled me close. Her arms went around me so snug I had a hard time pulling in a breath.

It was too much. This was the last time I would cry. Of course, I didn't know that then, but man did I bawl. There with my aunt, us turning together after that hug, to tap on Momma's door. Telling her all the good things about Aunt Linda and why we should stay together. You know, like how she read to me, how she was more like my sister than Momma's sister, how she kept good care of me.

Like that, Momma slammed the door open. It bounced on the wall and almost closed again. I stared at Momma. And it was like I was looking at her, seeing her, for the first time. She looked crazy. Wild-eyed. Hair a mess. Skin blotchy, red and white. Anger had changed her face to someone I almost didn't recognize.

"Get in your room." Momma's voice was a howl. I backed away, running into the oak railing that peeked over to the parlor below.

"What?"

"Now, Angela, calm down." Aunt Linda reached for Momma, who slapped her hands away.

"Go to bed, go to bed, go to bed!" Momma's voice deafened me.

"Go, Lacey." I almost couldn't hear Aunt Linda for the ringing in my ears.

"But . . ."

"Hurry." Again that almost whisper.

I moved down the hall, slow, unable to look away.

Momma took a step toward Aunt Linda. Her hands out. "It's three-fifteen. You have two hours," she said. "Then I'm calling the police." Momma stepped back into her room, slamming the door shut so hard I was surprised it didn't splinter in half.

And Aunt Linda left.

Packed her bags that night and high-tailed it outta our house. Told me in whispers she planned to stay in a hotel in Peace then pick up Mr. Dewey from the library as soon as she could. That she would call who she had to call. That she would make things right.

Just like that, she was gone.

Now my guts still tightened from the recollection. I tried to shake this heavy memory from my shoulders as I gripped the cart handle. "The only way to forget," I said to the books, "is to get to work."

So I started in the informational section, quick like I used to when I would help Aunt Linda, before. I piled the books on the shelves where they belonged, making the rows as neat as possible. In the background a mother read to her baby too young to even sit up. An ancient woman looked for something on the computer. Three little boys discussed horror stories at a round table in the center of the room.

I did my job and tried not to think of what still hurt to the quick.

My aunt leaving me.

I worked like a madman. Went through all those dinosaur books. The insects. Sharks.

The air conditioner flicked on, making the lights dim for a second. I tried hard not to remember the next part of that late night. The part of me running into the dew-covered grass, my legs getting damp from the calves right on down. The stars so bright. The sky not appearing at all the way I felt it should. You know, sad for what was happening in my house. What was happening to *me*.

What about you?

"Aunt Linda."

She was in her car by then. Her three suitcases piled up in the backseat.

She glanced at me, her face lit pale in the dashboard lights. "Lacey-girl. What are you doing following me? You're gonna catch a cold." She used her gentle reading voice there in the dark. So Momma wouldn't hear? Wouldn't wake up and call the police? "You don't want your mother to see you."

Goose bumps covered my arms and I rubbed the chill away.

"Where you going?" I had stood in Aunt Linda's bedroom doorway watching while she packed, even after Momma sent me to my room three different times, the last with a swat to the bottom—at my age.

But I had snuck out. I had to sneak out. Had to say good-bye.

"Where are you going?" I asked. A breeze pushed at oak leaves making them chatter.

"Now baby, I can't tell you that." Tears filled up Aunt Linda's eyes. For a moment I was sure they'd spill free, slide down her face, drip off her chin, maybe fall fall fall all the way to China. But those tears didn't fall. Not even when she gave a shrug.

"Why not?" Something jabbed at my insides.

Aunt Linda looked past the windshield of the car like the way she spoke of was up ahead. Though the engine was on, she'd left the lights off. She took in a deep breath, let her words escape with it. But it was like she spoke to herself. "I knew this was coming for a while now. I could see it coming." She shook her head. "I could see poor Angela getting lower. More depressed and anxious and afraid. Like before. You remember before, don't you, Lacey?" I nodded. "I tried to get her into the doctor, but she wouldn't have any of the pills he gave her." Aunt Linda squeezed the steering wheel. "I can't stand to see your mother like this. It's so hard to watch her. It's as though she's had our father sitting on her shoulder for the last few months. It's like he's pointing the directions she should go and she never hesitates." Aunt Linda took in a deep breath.

My feet were cold. A frog called for rain, and far away the sky lit up with a streak of silent lightning.

"She hates for me to talk of it, you know."

I nodded again but Aunt Linda wasn't looking at me. Just staring straight ahead. Into the dark. Quick, I looked that way, too. Checking.

For what?

There was nothing. Even the lightning bugs had gone to bed.

"Angela really hates for me to point to the things that aren't working. Or the fact that Daddy is gone and that he's been gone as long as you've been alive. She doesn't get it that we have to move on." Aunt Linda's voice was soft, like she was convincing herself, not just me. "She's not right. But you can't tell people that, can you?"

I shook my head. I mean, I'd known for years Momma

was not quite right. And that she'd been getting worse, little by little. Someone slipping over a steep ledge in slow motion.

"This whole thing," Aunt Linda waved a hand around like the yard had something to do with Momma's sadness, "this whole thing is dragging me down, too." From somewhere came the smell of pine and water. I heard a sandpiper cry out. "And Lacey, it's dragging you down. Don't think I haven't noticed."

Boy, the truth of that was a shovel to the head. All this time I felt like I was stuck in an ice cube. That no one saw me in all the trouble. But Aunt Linda had.

Her knowing this made me wild with worry at her going. Panic ran up my spine. Made me speak.

"Please don't go," I had said. And I reached in the car and touched her warm shoulder. Felt the shimmer of her shirt beneath my fingers. "Please. I'll beg her. I'll help with her more. I'll do better."

Aunt Linda's tears fell then. Green-colored light reflected in the wet path on my aunt's face.

"She won't let me stay. And she won't let me take you, Lacey," Aunt Linda said. She put the car in gear then, and took off, driving slow. I walked beside her. Fear worse than anything the thought Granddaddy *might* have caused took hold of me tight. "I begged her, Lacey. I told her that I would care for you. I've looked for two-bedroom places. I have."

Momma's voice cut through the night—a scream that sent the hair on the back of my neck straight up. "I've called the police. I've called the police and they're on their way."

"Momma," I said. I was so sad I thought I might follow my mother to the edge of the cliff where she seemed to be in her head. "Momma, please!"

"Get inside now, Lacey!"

"I've looked for a place for the both of us," Aunt Linda said. She peeked in the rearview mirror like she checked for Momma. But I could see my mother standing in the doorway at the front of the house, pale as a spirit.

"Okay." My pulse quickened at my possible going. I could do it. Go with Aunt Linda. Just check in with Momma. You know, make sure she was okay. I could live half with Momma, half with Aunt Linda. That would work! It would!

"It's kidnapping if I take you, she told me that," Aunt Linda said. She was quiet. "We've fought about this a lot. I even went to see a lawyer. I can't get you unless your momma is a harm to you or herself. Depression doesn't count."

"They said they'd be here in less than five minutes." Momma's voice was a scream. A neighbor's light went on.

"So stay," I said. Desperation clawed at me. Made it hard for me to see. "I'll talk to the police when they get here." I pulled at Aunt Linda's shirt to make the car stop going, to convince her to stay with me. "I'll hide you in my room. I got that big ol' walk-in closet. *I'll* sleep there. You can have the bed."

Aunt Linda gave this laugh that turned into a hiccup from all the silent crying she was doing. Had done.

"I've done everything I can, baby Lacey." She reached for my hand. I thought maybe she would hold on to me, but she pried my fingers away from her shirt.

I grabbed the door handle. "Don't go."

"You're killing me," she said.

"What will I do if you go?"

"I'll make the calls again. I'll call the state offices and tell them about your mom. I'll try to get you. Until then, you just call me if there's a problem, you hear? You know my cell phone number." And she moved forward faster, even though I held on to the car. Even though I jogged next to her, ignoring Momma's screaming. Out of the driveway. Down the street a bit.

"Let go, Lacey."

Me running for a moment. Feet slapping at the road. Passing two houses. One with their upstairs lights on.

"Let go."

I did.

And she left. Left me standing in the dark. The smell of car exhaust in the cold night air swirling around, drowning out the pine and water scent.

"What if I can't call?" I was crying too, though I discovered it right that second. Crying because I had thought she loved me enough to stay. No matter what. Even with the police. No matter what a lawyer said.

Except Aunt Linda was down the road now. All the way to the stop sign. She couldn't have heard me. Probably couldn't even see me anymore. But that's when the reverse lights came on. The engine whined as she backed up.

"I'll get an apartment," she said, full-out weeping. "I'll make sure it has two bedrooms. I have a friend who said I could have a job at the St. Augustine library. It's a pay raise even. More responsibility. They've promised it to me. That's only twenty minutes away by car, you know. If I can work things through, I'll get you over to my place."

Hoping, I said, "Really?"

She nodded.

"And maybe a place for Momma, too?" Because, even a year ago I knew I shouldn't leave her. At that point me and Aunt Linda couldn't leave Momma on her own. What in the world would she do all alone? If I went with Aunt Linda, I mean? What would Momma do?

Aunt Linda was quiet a moment, tears running down her face. "Lacey. Just call me if you need me. Or if your momma needs me. You promise?"

"Yes, ma'am," I said.

"I'll check on you. I'll stop by and see how you are. And I swear I'll make those phone calls again."

And she did come by. Three times. She was met by Momma with a breath of fire and words that stung. I watched from the window each visit, peered through the curtains. Saw and heard it all. The way Momma was. Saw the way my aunt cried. And when I tried to come outside that first visit, Momma had slapped me a good one right in the face, something she had never done before.

Then there was the last time. That awful last time. When Aunt Linda pulled into the drive and a few moments later the police arrived. Right in the middle of a Sunday afternoon. The whole neighborhood, it seemed, peering at us from behind curtains—some people coming right onto their front porches to watch us.

I had run outside that day. Run straight to Aunt Linda, who stood half in her car, half out.

"What's this?" she said.

Momma came outside, the screen door slamming behind her. "I told you, Linda," Momma said.

I glanced at her. Did a double take. Momma was dressed in her Sunday clothes, from before, when we used to go to church. She had on high heels and carried a purse that didn't match. She wore makeup. Her hair was brushed.

"Momma?" I said.

Momma moved to where I stood and put her arm around my shoulders. "Baby," she said, and her voice was soft. "Baby, she's not allowed to be here."

Aunt Linda got out of the car. A policeman and -woman got out of their cars. Someone nearby laughed. A mockingbird cried out. The sun was so hot. So hot.

With her arm around me, Momma marched up to the police. "I own this house," she said. "This is my girl." Momma squeezed me close. "And my sister, she wants everything. Including this child of mine." Momma swallowed at something. "She's tried to take Lacey from me."

"Momma," I said. The air was as still as a failed promise.

Aunt Linda hurried over. "I just want to visit with my niece. I just want to come to the home where I was raised."

"I have a restraining order," Momma said.

"What?" I said. And Aunt Linda said, "What?" too.

"I did it myself." Momma straightened her shoulders. "Went into the police station. Alone. Saw the judge, even." She smiled and I could see it wasn't quite real, that smile. It was almost see-through. Like glass. From her purse Momma pulled out some paperwork. Her hands shook. The papers shivered.

The lady cop glanced at them then handed it all back to Momma. "You can't be here, ma'am," she said. Her voice was gentle. Her face kind.

"But I love her," I said. The words came out like they were sorry.

Momma's grip tightened. "You love me, too," she said.

"I love you both," I said.

"Off my property, Linda," Momma said.

"Angela, please."

"Momma!"

The policeman came forward. "Tell her good-bye. Get permission to come back."

Aunt Linda was motionless. Her face grew pale and I saw her grit her teeth.

I ran to her. Threw my arms around her neck. Kissed her face. She tucked herself close.

And then she was escorted to her car.

But Aunt Linda and me, how could we know all that when she was driving off the first night Momma made her leave?

"Give me your word you'll call me, Lacey," she had said.

"I will," I had said.

Then I watched her go. I didn't grab at the car. Didn't run after her. 'Cause I knew it didn't matter. That it wouldn't matter what I did.

Aunt Linda wouldn't stay with me.

Funny thing happened right after the police left all that time later, and I remembered it now as I cleared the last of the cart off and started shelving the Clementine books in the juvenile fiction section.

Soon as she was escorted away from our home, soon as she drove away from me not looking back even once, I got all mad at my aunt. Walking into the house that afternoon, the police done talking to Momma, I went up to my room, fell on my bed and didn't leak one tear, not one, though the effort made my head hurt and my nose go stuffy.

Aunt Linda gone.

Gone.

Now it was just Momma and me. All alone here in Peace. All alone in this house. Granddaddy peering in at us— Momma was sure. Me feeling so achy inside. Not a bit of peace in my heart. Hating everyone, including my watchful, dead grandfather. And my aunt. And Momma, too. I hated them all.

"We made him happy," Momma said, coming in to pat my head. "Granddaddy is sure we've done the right thing."

I didn't answer. The police were long gone. Aunt Linda, too. Momma had put on more makeup, two red circles of blush high on her cheekbones, so much mascara her eyelashes looked spidery. She wore three sweaters though it was hot in the house. Tight and closed up.

"He told me so, Lacey," Momma said through purple-painted lips.

I wouldn't even look my mother in the face as she walked away, stood thin near my bedroom door. Pale light falling in on her from the hall. Teetering on her high heels. There was a run in her panty hose. Had it been there all along?

"You'd hear him too, if you'd just listen."

"I don't want to listen," I wanted to say. But I kept my lips glued shut. I waited for her to leave—the two of us standing there. Momma turned away first, went to her room.

When I heard Momma settle into bed, I stood in front of my dresser mirror. I whispered, "We don't need you, Linda Mills. We don't. We *don't*." I said the words over and over. Saying them would make them real. And I swore to myself, right then, I would never call her. Never.

Momma, all peaceful now, like nothing had happened, called from her room, "You okay, Lacey?"

And I lied to her. "Yes, Momma. I'm okay."

Momma didn't get out of bed for three days, except to drink sips of water and go to the bathroom. But we were okay.

VII

I worked hard trying to forget while I shelved all those books. But I couldn't. It was almost like Aunt Linda was a part of the books. Made of pages or something. Bits of words. And she had made me a part too, by reading to me. By holding me on her lap while she read. By kissing my cheek when she ended a chapter and closed a novel and tucked me in at night. It was like now she was some fairy from another world, trapped between the covers. And if I worked hard enough, or put the books away in just the right order, I might release her.

"Lacey Mills," I said. All these things, all these thoughts? Pure stupidity. "You are crazier than Momma."

You are! You are!

I held tight to the novels in my hands. I sighed, all the way from my toes.

Straight up I have to say, it's not Momma's fault she is the way she is. She's just scared. I blame Granddaddy and so did Aunt Linda, though Momma is the first to defend him. But who can help being afraid? Who can help missing her father, even if he wasn't perfect? Who isn't afraid of death?

That fall terrorists flew airplanes into the World Trade Center? I was at school. A little ol' thing. Aunt Linda was out of town at a librarian's meeting. Momma at home.

I knew, though. I knew, little as I was. If Momma was watching at home, we were in trouble. Big, big trouble. Why, I was watching the most horrible thing I'd ever seen in my life. If Momma was watching TV too, this would not be good for her.

The school wouldn't let me get home. Told me I had to stay right where I was. Just in case Florida got attacked, I guess. Made us practice getting under desks and everything.

I ran home from the bus stop that afternoon. My feet hitting the pavement like hands on a drum. My stomach sick from what I had seen. My heart all twisted up. Tears coming down my face.

And oh! was I right about Momma.

The house was silent when I opened the front door. All the lights on. I couldn't seem to find her anywhere. Not anywhere. Not on the first floor. Or near the washer and dryer on the back porch. Not in her room or Aunt Linda's.

At last, at last, I heard voices when I went into my bedroom. Saw my closet door opened just a crack. Could see the light was on. Shadows of people?

"Momma," I said, whispering. All day I'd sat with a lump the size of a grapefruit in my chest.

I opened the door wide. There she was on the floor in front of me, curled up on my shoes, Granddaddy's pictures pulled out around her. Even the portrait from the wall, the one where she was with him, his arm around her, it was there in the closet. In the photo Granddaddy and a younger Momma, side by side, looking almost like twins, their hair and eyes that same dark color. And that skin that won't tan, not even a bit. Smiling. The two of them smiling. That portrait leaned against her knee. Seeing her like that made me think, *Momma is okay. She is.*

"I seen Granddaddy," she said to me then. Didn't look at me. Just said those words. "Seen him right after the buildings fell. First he was in the smoke and glass from the buildings. Then standing in the living room."

Momma's been talking about her dead father ever since

I can remember. You know—about hearing his voice. And seeing him. Saying sometimes how the two of them talk late into the night so Momma has a hard time getting up in the morning. It used to scare me, but after a while I got used to it. I've never seen him, so why be afraid of a memory? Even if the memory talks to your mother?

"Momma," I had said. "Come on out of there." I reached in, my hand so small. I remember that, my hand being so small. I touched her dirty hair. My stomach twisted with the awful things I'd seen at school. The smell coming from the closet. The burning buildings. The sparkling glass. The smoke. The way Momma would be so upset about it. She'd been having a hard time for a few days anyway. Worrying, pulling at her hair, whispering to Granddaddy.

"He said," Momma said from the floor, "it's the end of the world. Said we should wait for the destruction. And save water. I ran the tub full, Lacey. And all the sinks, too." She spoke into her chest. Not looking up.

I was petrified anyway and for some reason Momma's words scared me even more that day. The picture—all the family pictures around her—were no longer soothing.

"Now, now," I said. Something Aunt Linda always said to her sister. But she was at that meeting. It was just me and Momma on September eleventh. Just the two of us. And my heart was broken from it all.

"Come on." I reached for Momma again and noticed my hands shaking.

"Can't."

"Come on now."

I reached for her and Momma glanced at me.

At first I thought maybe that wasn't my mother sitting there cross-legged near my shoes. That maybe someone had stolen her voice or something. Her face was so shiny in the sunlight that swept in from my bedroom window. And dark. I jerked away from her. And she made this smile. Like a carved pumpkin smile. With not a bit of happiness in it.

I realized then all the dark was blood. Her whole face covered in blood.

"What?" I said. "What?" For a moment I couldn't even move. I was a statue, poised in my bedroom closet. Then I stumbled backward, hitting my nightstand. Something fell to the floor and broke. And the sun kept shining and shining.

Momma cocked her head at me like a bird does when it gazes at you. "Oh, this?" She touched her cheek and shrugged. "I don't know." Her voice was light, almost floaty.

For a minute I was sure I was gonna throw up. I mean, all those people dead that morning. All those people gone. All that fear. The way I felt. And Momma looking up at me. The blood. I gagged. Turned my back. Gagged again.

"Get out of the closet." Now, looking back, I'm not sure how I even got those words out.

"Lacey." Momma's voice was a whine.

"Now." Then I threw up. All over the wooden floor. Vomit splashing up on the wall. And on the small rug where I knelt to say my prayers. And I cried, too. For everything that had happened that awful, awful day. Tell me who wasn't upset that day? Or afraid?

"Lacey?" John's voice pulled me back into the library. "How's Linda doing?"

For a minute I couldn't figure what John was talking about, I was so back there on September eleventh.

I stood up, blinking. "Oh, she's doing good." Not a lie, really, but I had no idea what was going on with my aunt. I hadn't seen her since she left, except those times from the window. And with the police. There was the letter, too. But nothing else. I hadn't tried to call her at all. Okay, I did twice, but the phone went to voice mail. Probably because I had called at like two in the morning, both times after Granddaddy had awakened Momma. "Yes, she's good."

"She seems to be," John said. "The whole library loves it when she stops in."

"What?" My face went flat. The floor tilted. "She visits here?" For some reason my hands shook. I clutched the handle of the book cart.

"She used to come a couple times a month hoping that Mr. Dewey would be returned," John said. "We've haven't seen her in a while." He peered over my shoulder at the almost-empty third cart. "Looks like you're about finished here. We've got new DVDs and CDs that need to be unwrapped when you're done."

"All right, John," I said. But in my head the words came out slow and fat, like bold print might sound.

He smiled big at me. "Lacey, it's nice to have you here. You look a lot like your aunt."

"Thank you." I nodded. "That's nice. I'm glad to be here."

Mr. Dewey returned? What did that mean?

After the videos and CDs were unwrapped. After I'd dusted things. After I'd helped a little girl find her older brother, I stood at the back of the children's section. Here, two large windows, floor to ceiling, looked out at the Peace River, which was nearly a mile across at this point. In the distance was a dark line of green, the other shore. Past that, the ocean. South down the coast a ways, St. Augustine.

"You've been in town and not stopped to see me," I said at the river. I was too shocked to feel pain, though I knew it was in there somewhere. Trying to find a place to hide in the memories, maybe.

I stood at the window a long time. Thought of Aunt Linda's reaction when she came home a few minutes after I got Momma out of the closet. Her finding us in the kitchen, me dabbing at the blood with a damp dish towel. Aunt Linda freaking out. Us finally getting it out of Momma that she had scratched most of the skin from her face because Granddaddy had said it would keep her safe.

Now I hugged myself and looked at the water, the way the sun made bright little chips of light on the surface.

"Momma," I said under my breath, "I hope this Winn-Dixie job is good for you. You got to get better."

"She needs help," Aunt Linda had said, bandaging Momma up. "You need help, Angela."

But Momma had just smiled. Both Aunt Linda and me, we tucked Momma into bed, kissing the side of her head.

None of us ever talked about that incident again. Momma didn't go for help. But she did kick Aunt Linda out.

Momma and me alone at the house in the city of Peace. With Granddaddy telling her what to do. And me cleaning up after it all.

You need help, Angela. Lacey—you *need help.*

And I did. I did. I squeezed my eyes shut.

"Hey."

I almost jumped out of my skin at the voice. Turning, I saw Aaron.

"You scared me," I said.

"Isn't it time for you to go home?" he said.

92

For a moment I stood at the edge of the library, tucked full into the memory of my family and their craziness.

I glanced at the clock. "Yeah, it looks like it. Have to pick my momma up at the Winn-Dixie pretty soon."

Aaron showed his crooked teeth in a small smile. His forehead was sweaty.

"I'll go with you then. We're headed the same way."

With me, I thought. With me sounded good. Me not alone if he went *with* me.

You need help.

"Okay, that'd be real nice," I said. We walked from the children's section of the library, waving good-bye to John. One last time I looked around.

Oh, Aunt Linda.

VIII

While we waited at the bus stop, Aaron let me try his skateboard. I was pretty bad. And thumping around in my head was the thought of Aunt Linda so close and never stopping to see me. It made me ache all over. Even my skin felt funny. Like I had the flu or something.

"It's okay, Lacey," Aaron said. He touched me on the elbow with a finger. "I'll teach you how if you want. We've got the summer." He smiled. "I'm a pretty good teacher."

My mind was full of excuses. Full of Momma. Of responsibility. Of no Aunt Linda.

"Not really," I said.

"Not really what?" In the sun and heat of the day, Aaron squinted at me.

Clack, clack, clack, said his skateboard on the sidewalk.

We stood near the concrete bench, waiting. I squinted too and stared off down the road. I could see the bus coming, just an ant of a thing. I shrugged at nothing.

What should I say? I didn't want this little bit of time to be over. Without meaning to, I liked Aaron. He was nice. Like a gift. He had appeared from nowhere, someone to be my friend after summers of no friends. After months of nothing but Momma.

Still, I knew sure as beets that my time was twisted tight in Momma's fists.

"I have this job." I motioned to the library behind us. "Five days a week. While my momma's working at the Winn-Dixie."

I have Momma, I thought. *I have to watch her. Care for her. Pat away her sadness.*

Aaron looked off to the bus that chugged closer, stopping off down the road from us. The afternoon sun played on the gold in his hair. He shrugged. "So you come a little earlier. Or we stay a little later. I mean, if you want." He paused. "Do you want to?"

A part of me *did* want to.

A part of me was scared of skateboarding.

Of being away from home too much.

Still.

"I'm not real sure. I *think* it'd be fun. Let's talk to Momma when she gets on the bus."

"Okay." He was quiet a moment.

"Yeah," I said, a bit of excitement coming up into my stomach. It burned out to my palms. "Yeah. That would be fun. Let's see what she says." I smiled, feeling almost what normal used to feel like.

For that second, I was free.

I shrugged again. So what, I had thought about Aunt Linda so much? So what? I didn't need her. It was Momma and me. And on the side it could be me learning to skateboard. With Aaron.

The thought was round and soft in my head. I couldn't help but smile again.

A dad with two small children hurried to the bench to wait with us.

"Bus is coming," said the littlest. She jumped up and down on one foot, her curls bouncing. "Bus is coming."

"You know, I could come to your house," Aaron said. "You wouldn't have to leave at all. We could skate out on the street."

"Maybe," I said. Could it be true? Could someone—a guy even—want to do something with me?

His face turned pink. He drummed on his knees like he heard a song I didn't.

The bus stopped in front of us. With a belch the doors opened. Several people stepped off and hurried away. The man and his two kids got on first.

And Aaron? He started talking and didn't stop. Even with that pink face, he didn't stop talking. I was full of wonder at the way he kept going. I would have never been able to pursue a thing—whatever it might be—the way he did. Words would pile up on my tongue then get trapped back behind my teeth. But not him. He didn't even need answers from me.

"The road's not bad down there. Pretty smooth. A pebble here and there, but mostly not. And with all the shade trees, well, there's places to rest. I built a ramp. Have you seen it?" He looked at me.

I nodded.

"Yeah, my dad and me, we built that ramp out of scraps I found. That took us a good long time. He drives a truck and he's not always home."

Glancing around the bus, I looked for Tattoo Guy. He wasn't there. I sat down in the front seat and Aaron plopped right next to me, his skateboard making a slapping sound when he dropped it to the floor. He put his feet on it and they rolled this way and that with the bus's movement.

We were close enough to touch, Aaron and me. His arm,

warm from the sun, kept brushing against mine. Three knuckles were skinned up, almost like Momma's face that September day so long ago. I looked away.

Get it out, that thought. Get it out!

I didn't want to think about Momma. I wanted to just be me. Me with a boy who would teach me to skateboard if I wanted. And with a nervous feeling creeping down from my scalp, I knew I *did* want to learn. This was so exciting, I couldn't believe it was possible.

I was making a friend.

Out the corner of my eye, I looked at Aaron. He laid his head back on the seat.

How was my breath? All day working in the library, thinking sad thoughts, breathing in the smell of books. Did my breath smell like something published before 1950 and left on the shelf all those years? What did my whole *self* smell like?

Real casual, I made like I was wiping sweat from my top lip and sniffed at my armpits. Not too bad. And I could always keep my arms pinned to my sides if necessary.

"Think your mom'll let you?"

Aaron's voice surprised me. Had he seen me sniffing? I jerked my head to him so fast I popped my own neck.

"She might," I said. And why not? Today was going to be different. *Was* different already. "She just might."

We rode in silence awhile, me grinning like crazy on the inside. Thrill about to overwhelm me. It was sort of hard to breathe.

"We're just about to Winn-Dixie," Aaron said. He leaned forward in his seat, pushing his hair behind his ear, then stared out the window. He gestured with his head and his tucked-in hair fell free.

I looked out the window to the dirty bus stop. Only two people stood at the bench there. An ancient woman and an ancient-er man. Between them was a small silver pushcart full of groceries. The woman's dress, flowered and past her knees, rippled in the breeze.

For a moment I couldn't think. It was like someone had drawn a line through my thoughts, x-ed them out. Left me blank on the inside.

And then . . . "Momma?"

I got to my feet. It felt like a fist pounded my nerves. I pulled the line even though the bus was coming to a halt.

Where was she? Where was my mother? She should be out with the old people. She should have bags of groceries to take home. She should be smiling, waiting for me to get her.

The whole bus stop seemed to go black and white. Right before my eyes. My breathing came so fast I thought I might faint dead away.

I grabbed hold of the bar to steady myself as the bus

lurched to a stop. Straining, I looked at the few people coming and going at the doors of the Winn-Dixie. None of them was my mother. None of them. All the sudden I felt sick to my stomach. Like I might throw up. I could feel vomit sitting at the top of my throat.

"What's the matter?" Aaron said.

"She's not here." My voice was almost a cry of pain. My eyes felt buggy. I looked at the Payless shoe store, and the pizza parlor, and the Time Kept watch repair shop.

In slowest motion, the old man and woman dragged their cart onto the bus. I stepped to the opposite window, flattened my hands on the glass, and looked for Momma. She was nowhere to be seen. The bus doors hissed closed.

"Wait," I said. My voice came out louder than I meant it to. My heart hurt, that's how hard it hammered in my chest. "Wait. Let me off." And then I was moving. I stumbled up to the driver, catching myself on the Plexiglas behind him. "Let me off now, please."

"All right, all right. Take it easy," the driver said. He glanced at me in the mirror, his eyebrows scrunched together. The doors swooshed open and I leapt from the top step, just about falling into the road when I landed on the ground.

Pound, pound, pound went my heart. The bus roared away, and the smell of exhaust burned.

My eyes teared up.

Momma. Momma. Please be working overtime. Please be loving this job. Please.

"Don't worry, Lacey," Aaron said. I hadn't realized he was here. With me.

Not along. Not.

"I'll look for her with you. We'll find her." He touched my forearm with his fingertips.

I couldn't say anything. This was bad. This was *bad.* I knew that without even knowing what had happened.

She's gone. You let her get away. Selfish.

No! I ran across the hot parking lot. Behind me I heard the skateboard hit the ground. Aaron rode up. I'd never run so fast. My hair flying back. Sweat on my upper lip. Under my arms.

Selfish.

"No." This time the word escaped from me. My tongue felt fat. Too big for me to swallow.

Momma, where are you? Calm down. Calm down. Maybe, just maybe, she was in the store. But somehow—from my clenched stomach?—I knew she wasn't.

Just take a deep breath. A deep cleansing breath. The smell of the black asphalt filled my nose. The scorching sun beat down. The air felt like a wet blanket. When had it gotten so hot? A car beeped somewhere behind me. Another car answered.

"I'm not late," I said out loud. "I know I'm not late." My voice shook.

For a moment I remembered the two weeks after Aunt Linda left. I squeezed my eyes tight at the thought.

"Please," I said, but without any sound. "Not that again."

It all came back to me in a flash—like lightning. How Momma wouldn't be waiting in her room when I got home from school. How I would look for her and find her sitting on the neighbor's lawn, them not even home from work. Or walking along the road leading into town, wearing only one shoe and her housecoat. Or in the tree near my bus stop.

One day—I shivered just thinking of it—I looked for Momma all over the house. I walked the neighborhood. I called and called for her. And that afternoon as the sun set, when I was ready to phone the police, I collapsed on the front porch, crying.

"What is it, girl?" I heard her voice, muffled. Sounding far away, almost.

"Momma?" I had said.

"What are you crying for, baby?"

I burst into tears then. Started sobbing.

"Momma, where are you?"

I came to the edge of the porch and looked out over the property. Out through the oaks that grew strong and tall, Spanish moss dripping from the limbs. I looked out toward the old garage that housed Momma's car that we hadn't driven for months now. Out into the near darkness and called for her.

"Where are you off to?" I had said.

"I'm right here, Lacey."

Momma's hand reached from below my feet, that slender arm of hers snaking up after it.

I screamed till I saw light flash behind my eyelids. I screamed till I thought my voice might break.

"I been here all along, Lacey," Momma said, from under the porch

"Get out!" I screamed at her. "Get out from under there, Momma. There's snakes under the house, you know that."

Momma pulled herself from under the old wooden porch. Dead leaves stuck to her nightgown, cobwebs were in her hair. But lucky for her she wasn't bitten by a snake.

"Momma," I said, brushing dirt from her face. "Momma, you know better than that. We've seen rattlesnakes in this yard. We've seen coral snakes. What in the world were you thinking?"

Momma shrugged. "Granddaddy told me to," was all she said.

But that was over—all her running off. Ten months ago, at least, she stopped her running. She stayed home so I could go to school without worry. She didn't bother the neighbors, didn't peer in their windows, didn't climb in their cars. It was done with. I had been sure.

But you aren't sure now.

"I know I'm not late," I said to Aaron. I looked him right in the eye and he looked back at me. "We said four-thirty."

"What?"

"I was supposed to meet her at four-thirty."

"Oh." He nodded. "I get it."

Into the store I ran, the air-conditioning making me feel damp where I had sweated. The smell of greasy chicken filled the air. A girl who pushed grocery carts in line glanced at me, then away.

"Maybe your mom decided to work a little extra," Aaron said, jogging close, skateboard tucked under his arm. "My mom comes home from work late lots of times."

"Maybe," I said. "I hope so." I stopped and looked at all the checkers, searching for Momma's shiny hair. Her thin body. Twig fingers. "She's not at any of the stands."

So we hunted, Aaron and me. Near the fruits and vegetables, up and down all the aisles, in the meat section—the whole time my heart beating harder or not at all. I swear, it felt like sometimes it stopped. When I realized I had lost her, it just quit. Momma wasn't in any of those places. In fact, she wasn't in the store period. I know because we checked the break room and the huge storage room in the back and both bathrooms.

Momma was gone.

You lost her, Lacey. You!

"How about I look around the outside of the store?" Aaron said.

"That's a good idea." I was having trouble getting spit down. My body was shutting off, one organ at a time. Like on TV. Like on those rescue shows where people died and weren't rescued at all. "She's got on a red checker's apron. And her hair is long. And black. And pulled back."

Aaron nodded.

"She's not that tall. Just about an inch more than me. And she's thin." For some reason, saying she was thin bit at my insides. She was *too* thin, I wanted to say, but didn't.

"It's okay, Lacey," Aaron said. "I saw her on the bus. I've seen her at your house. I think I'll recognize her." He moved close to my face and I could smell the penny smell of sweat on him. Could see part of his bangs stuck to his forehead. "We're gonna find her." He patted at my shoulder.

"You're right. I've got to think that." But I couldn't make my mind think anything positive. Where Momma was concerned there was only worry.

Aaron hurried toward the door.

I went up to the service desk.

The lady behind the counter smiled. Her name tag read EMMA. "Yes?"

"I've lost my mother."

"What's her name, honey? I'll page her."

"No," I said, wringing my hands, trying to warm them. Even in the heat I was freezing. "I've already looked everywhere. She's not in the store. She's not here."

"Then I can't help you."

Overhead came the voice of a man advertising green beans and canned corn that was on sale today only.

I leaned toward Emma. Her eyebrows, I saw, were painted on. Her left ear was filled with earrings. "She was here earlier, though. I dropped her off. She came in to work. To work for you."

Emma's eyes went large. "Let me get the manager," she said.

There was a bench by the service desk, a golden oak one. I sat down while Emma called for the manager. Smells of French bread and fresh-baked cookies and garlic floated over from the deli. The fluorescent lights buzzed. I realized I was hungry, though I'm not sure I could have eaten a bite, the way I felt tied up like a knot. I waited, praying the words "Please help me find her," again and again.

The manager was named Alfred, though he looked way too young to have that name. Emma talked to him a moment, then Alfred walked over to where I sat.

It was kind of like in the movies, the way he came up. You know, getting bigger and bigger with each step. Me feeling the blood race through my neck. I stood, my mouth dry. Heard Aaron walk up beside me.

"You're Angela's daughter?"

I nodded.

Alfred said, "She left less than an hour after she got here. Quit."

I opened my mouth twice, trying to get the word out. "Quit?"

Oh. No.

IX

"She was . . ." Alfred stumbled around for words. ". . . she was pretty upset."

"I see," I said. "I see. Okay then." But it wasn't okay. It wasn't at all.

I wanted to shout at Alfred. I wanted to holler at him. To say, "You should have stopped her. You should have kept her here. Kept her safe." Wasn't that his duty? To make sure his employees were happy and stayed at their jobs and . . .

But even as the thoughts tumbled in my head I knew

they were wrong. Why, *I* couldn't keep Momma home and safe. And I knew her.

My bottom lip trembled a little. If I wasn't careful I might just scream. It was like I could feel a scream wanting to come out.

"Use the service phone," Alfred said. "Call home and see if she went on without you." Then he said, "I'm real sorry. She seemed awful distraught, that one."

I nodded, though I knew it was useless. It took me three failed tries before Aaron dialed home for me. And then the phone just rang. On and on. Thirty times I let the phone ring. Then I hung up.

"She's not there," I told Aaron. My voice was half a whisper.

Now he patted my elbow. His touch was awkward. But it gave me a bit of courage.

I could do this.

You can't.

I could! I *always* did it.

I ran up and down that little shopping strip, looking through every store over and over for I don't know how long. Then Aaron and I stood in front of the Winn-Dixie, neither one of us saying a word. In the distance, storm clouds piled up high. White on the top, and dark gray at the bottom. The air was heavy and still and smelled of cars and summer heat.

"Okay," I said. "Okay." My backpack rested on the ground beside me, leaning against my leg. I twisted my hands till they hurt. Bit my nails till one bled. "Now it's possible that she went home."

Aaron cleared his throat and I looked over at him, though he never took his eyes off the clouds building in the east.

"Lacey," he said. "If my mom went home, it'd be no big deal. I mean, she goes home all the time without me."

"Yes, yes, I understand." Though I didn't really. A momma who went home on her own?

"Maybe you're worrying about your mom a little too much. Maybe she's fine."

I couldn't speak at first. Anger boiled up into my brain. What did Aaron know? Nothing. Nothing at all!

That's right, a calmer me thought. *Nothing at all.* How could he know my momma?

"She doesn't think so good sometimes," I said after moment. "I kinda have to take care of her."

He gave a half nod. Standing right there next to me, Aaron was a good three inches taller than I was. Something Momma would have been proud of. She always says to me when we're sitting in my bedroom, the curtains pulled over the windows to keep out the light, "A boy oughta be taller than you, Lacey. Yes, he oughta."

"My momma . . ."

Could I tell him? Could I tell this boy about Momma not getting out of bed on some days, or cutting herself, or crying for hours and hours? Or about the nights she didn't sleep at all, and kept me up talking? How she was deathly afraid of birds because they meant death to her—any kind—even hummingbirds. Or how some days she was so upset, so afraid, that Aunt Linda had had to destroy all the credit cards because Momma went through Granddaddy's money so fast trying, hoping, to keep us safe?

No, that was too much. Way too much.

"I mean," I said, taking in a deep breath, "I mean, my momma's sick."

That's what Aunt Linda had said. Momma was sick. And getting worse. But I didn't tell Aaron *that*. I didn't tell him how Aunt Linda said Momma was killing herself a bit at a time. He wouldn't get it. Not unless he lived at my place. He just wouldn't get it.

He *wouldn't get it?* You *don't get it.*

So true. So true.

"We better find her then," Aaron said. Like that. He said it just like that.

The *we* again. That word made me feel sad. *We.* Momma, Aunt Linda, and me. We.

"Won't your momma be wanting you home?" I asked, making the words cotton-soft.

"I'll call her. It'll be okay."

Something kind of weird happened to me right then. I mean, I know I wasn't handing the burden of Momma over to anyone, but I was sharing it. It's not like I wasn't worried, I still was. But the worry didn't seem so heavy.

Aaron walked over the pay phone to call his momma because his cell phone had died. And I stood there thinking, *What if I hadn't said something to him on the bus? What if I had stayed mad and told him to leave me alone?*

Alone. That's the way I'd be doing things now if I had done something stupid earlier—like telling Aaron to stay with Tattoo Guy.

Aaron showing up was a miracle.

That's what Momma woulda said. "Lookit here, Lacey. Macaroni and cheese, six for a dollar. And right when we need it, too. It's a miracle."

In the distance, lightning played out in the darkened sky. A huge storm was coming.

Wasn't someone showing up just as good as six-for-a-dollar macaroni?

Yes. Yes, it was.

Maybe there'd be a miracle for me with Momma. I crossed my fingers.

Aaron hurried back. "I checked in," he said. "Let's get going."

"Maybe my momma *is* home," I said. "Or walking in the house right this very minute. We can catch the bus and look for her on the way."

"Good idea," he said.

Now hot air pushed across the parking lot picking up garbage and swirling it in small whirlwinds. We stood at the bus stop waiting. I glanced around, hoping, somehow, that Momma would show up. Pop out from behind some van and say, "Surprise, Lacey! I saw you looking for me. You sure did seem scared. Here I am!"

If that happened, I swear I wouldn't even be mad. I'd grab her in a hug around the neck and say, "Momma. You scared me something awful. I thought sure you'd left me." And then I'd say, "Lookit here, Momma. I made a friend." And I would introduce her to Aaron.

But Momma wasn't the playing-around kind. Not by a long shot. She'd never do anything like that.

Wandering off? That *had* been her.

Surprising me with something good? *Not* her.

Hurting herself? Her.

Thinking about what might make things easier for me. Not her.

But that wandering stuff only happened a few times. And she never went far from home. She did stuff as weird, though.

Like stocking up on tuna because we were gonna be in a terrible war any day now. Or washing all the clothes in the kitchen sink because Granddaddy had told her back in the olden days that's the way real women did the laundry. Or cutting her long, beautiful nails down so short they bled.

"I bet you your mom's waiting for you at the house," Aaron said. The hot breeze moved his hair like a ghost, lifting it, pushing it back with an invisible hand. "You want to call her again? See if she's made it yet?"

I looked away.

"She won't answer," I said after a moment. "Even if she is at home, she won't answer." I'd known that in the store.

"Why not?"

A truck passed in front of us, kicking up a pile of dust and clanging as it drove over a bump.

"She . . ." Still I didn't look at him. Should I say, "She's afraid. Afraid someone listens in on the line. Afraid someone is checking to see if she's alone. Afraid Granddaddy will call"? ". . . she just won't answer."

"Well, I bet she's waiting for you," Aaron said. "She's probably all worried about you."

"I sure hope so," I said. Oh and I did. I hoped that with all my heart. All my body parts. Everything that was me.

Please God. Please dear God. Those are the words that ran

through my head the whole time we waited for that bus. Every once in a while a wave of I'm-gonna-puke-my-guts-out filled me. *Momma. Oh Momma. Please dear God. Please.*

Right when the bus pulled into view, Aaron dropped his skateboard and grabbed ahold of my hands. His fingers tangled together with mine. He pulled me toward him a little, till we were face to face, looking right at each other.

"Lacey," he said. "It's all gonna be all right."

I stared into his eyes. Candy eyes. And I made myself believe his words. This boy that went to my school. This boy who lived not too far from me. This miracle boy, the way he showed up on the day I would need him. How could that be? Nothing ever worked out for me like that.

So I made myself believe Aaron. Ignored the feeling in my stomach and heart and believed. Because that's what you do with a miracle. You believe in it.

Together we climbed on the Peace City bus and rode back toward my house. My almost-normal feeling was gone. I was miles from ordinary now. Miles. Every once in a while Aaron patted at my hand. And each time, when tears threatened, I believed instead, even this far from what was usual.

I watched for Momma the whole way.

Anytime I saw someone wearing red, I made ready to leap to my feet and pull the wire that would get me off the bus and to my mother.

While I watched, Aaron and I talked about school. About how glad he was for the summer. About how his younger sisters, who were twins, had been a surprise to the family.

"My dad sure was happy," Aaron said. He let out a sigh that showed me he was happy, too.

In case he was gonna ask about my own father, I glanced out the window. My momma and daddy split long before I was born. According to Momma, Granddaddy hadn't wanted my daddy around.

"And your granddaddy made quick business of that," Momma told me once when Aunt Linda was still home.

Aunt Linda had nodded.

"He *was* jealous of the boys, wasn't he?"

"Yes, Angela, he was," Aunt Linda had said. She let out a laugh. "Remember how we met up with Daniel and that one guy—what was his name?"

Momma gave me a knowing look. "Daniel is your daddy, Lacey," she had said, matter-of-fact.

"Matthew Riley," Aunt Linda said. "We met up with Daniel and Matthew in St. Pete. Remember that?"

Momma nodded all solemnlike. "We told Granddaddy we were off to a rival football game. And he let us go. Worked our butts off, he did, but he let us go."

Aunt Linda said nothing for a minute. "Then he followed us, straight over to that old King's Pizza place."

"Uhm-hmm."

I listened back and forth. Not wanting to interrupt. Not even breathing, it seemed. Waiting to find out this something I had never known before. Never heard before. This something about my very own daddy.

Momma laughed then. Threw back her head and laughed. "We hadn't even taken a sip of Coke," she said between gasps, "when Daddy walked into that restaurant."

Now Aunt Linda laughed, too. "Their faces," she said. "Everyone's faces."

"What?" I said, daring a word. "What happened?"

Momma and Aunt Linda were laughing so hard that they fell onto to each other on the couch. Held each other up.

"Daddy," Momma said, and like that she was crying and laughing at the same time. And I saw that Aunt Linda was, too. "He came in with a shotgun. The whole room went quiet. Dead quiet." Momma wiped at her eyes.

"Are you kidding?" I said. "Are you kidding?"

"He made us both get into the truck," Aunt Linda said. "Right that very second, he made us get up from the booth. He told those boys we were his and drove us right on out of there." Aunt Linda's laughter had settled some. "I didn't ever see Matthew again," she said. "You sure can't blame him, though." Then she and Momma were rolling all over themselves again.

"I don't think that's funny," I said. "Not at all."

When they quieted some, Aunt Linda said, "He ran off every one we brought here to the house."

Momma looked over my head.

"Every one."

When I thought the story was done, my momma said, soft as a flower, "I sure did love my Daniel boy."

And that was that. Neither Momma nor Aunt Linda knew where he was now. His family packed up. Moved on away. But not before he got Momma pregnant.

Being daddy-less was one more thing that made me see my life wasn't a thing like anyone else's.

Especially at school.

As we bounced along on the bus, I told Aaron I didn't like school. That I didn't know Jace Isom from class that well. But it was a lie. A bold-faced lie.

"You sure? He has way long hair? And he hung out with me and my friends during lunch? He's a bad ass."

I shook my head no. As we drove farther from town, the bus thinned of people. Not too many families live out in the boonies like we do. "I've seen Jace plenty," I said. "Heard him in class. But I don't *know* him."

"Hmm," Aaron said. He nodded like he was thinking of how to convince me that I did, really, know Jace Isom.

"He pointed you out to me. Talked about you."

My heart thumped. I could hardly stand to think of this. Hardly bear to remember. Class. Me looking. Like Vickie did. Like Alison. Not saying a word. Thinking I might, thinking I maybe—in another life—that I might have the courage.

And Jace, walking right up to me. Right into my space. The wind blowing outside a bit. The summer almost here, May halfway over.

The girls watching. One of them giggling behind her hand.

And Jace stopping right there in front of me and saying, "You crazy or what? Why are you looking at me? Why?"

"Umm."

"You're ugly and stupid." He leaned close. "And crazy."

Behind him Vickie and Alison laughed louder.

"You hear me? Don't look at me anymore. You're giving me the creeps."

"I won't," I had said.

That day I walked home. Tears coming down my face. Me not making a sound.

But I kept my promise and didn't look in Jace's direction again.

Now the sun splashed through the bus window. Beside me, Aaron said nothing.

"What did he tell you?" The words seemed thin as butterfly wings. I took my eyes off the road long enough to give Aaron a glance. Now *he* stared out the window. "What did he say?"

"Stuff."

And there it was again. The differences. I knew they were coming. *Breathe easy. Take slow breaths.* "Like what? Bad things?" *Thump-thump* my heart said. "What kind of stuff?"

What was I doing? Why did I care what anyone thought? Why did I have to know?

For a moment Aaron didn't say anything. Then, "He said that you're always alone. That you don't have friends." He shrugged. "That you made out with him and that he dumped you."

"What?" I shook my head. Made out? "Not true. Not true."

Part is. You were alone, no friends. None. Alone.

Again Aaron was quiet. "Lacey, I've heard people talking where we live. I've seen a few things."

A few things?

My face turned hot. I knew what he was talking about. What people whispered at school about me. I knew they said I was weird, how I sometimes napped during class. How everybody should stay away from me. But I hadn't known the mean things had seeped out of my classroom to the other ninth grades.

"You don't have to look for Momma with me." It was all I could say. It felt like embarrassment colored my whole body bright red. Colored my words. Even my thoughts felt hot. But when I stared down at my hands I saw they were their normal color, though white at the knuckles.

What had he seen? What did he know?

I didn't want to imagine. But my mind ran ahead. Maybe, just maybe, Momma had been on Aaron's lawn. Maybe he had seen her wandering in the neighborhood. Maybe he had even heard her cries in the night. Had he seen her in her nightgown? Seen me trying to help her up the steps when she cried so she couldn't even stand?

Those houses were down the road from us a bit.

"Lacey." Aaron shrugged. "It's no big deal. I don't give a crap about what people say."

Sure, I thought. "I had a friend before," I said.

He nodded. His eyes were so brown.

Did he know how *that* ended? The memory of that sleepover brought tears to my own eyes all these years later. For a moment I was back in the middle of that night, shivering in the cold.

I sure wasn't going to say anything about that. How

Laurel had come to my house to spend the night. How Momma had freaked out early in the morning before the sun came up. How she pulled us both out of bed and made us stand outside in February cold while she searched the house, carrying a crucifix and a flashlight, looking for evil spirits.

Aunt Linda made things right that early morning. She fixed Laurel and me huge cups of homemade hot chocolate, thick with real cream. Tried to make a game of it. She calmed Momma down. Got us back in bed. Even took Laurel to her front door that next day after we slept in and explained things.

But at school the following Monday, Laurel told everyone what had happened.

I was horrified. It felt like the skin might bubble right off my bones.

"Don't," I had said. I remember I had reached out to stop Laurel, but never laid a hand on her. Just waved in her direction. Then sat in my desk, my head on the desktop, and waited for the telling to be over.

She wouldn't stop. Laurel told it again and again. About her momma being so angry and yelling at my momma. Momma was wrapped in an old coat of Granddaddy's, the winter wind pulling at her hair. She never said a word. Didn't even nod. And Laurel's momma kept on how she was gonna sue if Laurel came down with even a runny nose. All this in the front yard near the mailbox in voices so loud that neighbors' lights had popped on.

That was in fourth grade. I'd had a friend for almost one whole week.

I glanced at Aaron. "I had a friend before."

Maybe he knew that, too.

X

As soon as I saw my house, windows curtained like blind eyes, I knew Momma had been here.

I leapt off the bus.

She had been here, but she was gone. She had to be gone now. The front door stood open a little, like maybe the wind had pushed it wide enough for a glance inside. The lights were on—I could see that from where I stood with Aaron on the blacktop road that would be good for skateboarding. Light peeked out around the edges of the living room curtains.

My stomach sunk.

None of this was like Momma. Not the lights on or the door open or the traveling alone. I mean, before I had found her when she wandered off. I had found her, most of the time, right away.

And she was always close. She hardly ever left the neighborhood.

You took her away.

I did. I had. I took her away. Led her from the safety of our home.

"That house," she had said after I found her standing in a neighbor's yard, pointing at their home, "that's right where the old barn was. Where generations of Millses kept fishing boats and garden tools and tractors."

And once . . .

"The place he had that car parked? There was an oak big as Florida right there. Me and our cousins and Linda, we'd climb to the top, look through the trees to the river."

And once . . .

"It used to be wasn't nothing out here but the old sand road. Nothing fancy. Nothing new. I walk that blacktop road and I don't feel nothing of my old life. Just the eyes of the neighbors."

It was true. All the changes. Aunt Linda had sold off part of the land. One-acre parcels to ten people. And they'd put a real road here not that long ago. Maybe three, four years ago. And their houses followed.

When the homes popped up I said, "Momma, you can't go off like this now that we have people so close." And she had stopped. She had. And she had always been so close. Not including after Aunt Linda. But most always before. And most always after. She was right under my nose. Really.

Now looking at our house, I almost forgot how to exhale.

Near a set of cinder blocks stacked at the corner to keep our home off the ground, I got down on my hands and knees. The wind pushed at me, blowing leaves across the yard. The air was hot, even next to the grass.

I pretended for a minute that Aaron wasn't here. Wasn't watching me.

"Momma?" I called.

I could see some old cane poles lying close. Could see the funnel-shaped homes anteaters made. There was a stack of rusted tools, a shovel and two rakes, piled where a hand could reach them if needed. But it didn't seem anyone had been under the house that shouldn't have been.

"Well," I said, like this was something I did. I stood. Dusted the sand from my knees. Patted my hands together like I was shaking off flour.

Aaron looked at me big-eyed.

I stared back.

"She hid there once," I said. Just gave it to him, that bit of me.

"I see," he said. But I could tell he didn't.

I took small steps and Aaron followed, setting his skateboard on the gray wooden porch.

"I think she's home," Aaron said. "Maybe inside. The door's open. And see the lights?"

"Yeah," I said.

To tell the truth, right at that moment I did *not* want to go inside. To tell the truth, I'd rather crawl around *under* the house. Take my chances with the rattlers and coral snakes. Instead, I pushed at the front door and it squeaked open like maybe it felt the same as me: scared.

In the living room I said, "Oh no." Something like despair grew heavy in my stomach. "This isn't good."

I had to steady myself on an ancient phone table. Thought I might fall.

"What?"

"*All* the lights are on. Even the night-lights."

"I noticed that," Aaron said.

The living room was wiped clean. There was no dust in here. No breeze from outside. The windows were latched shut. The lace at the glass, breaking the outside into small pieces, like a puzzle—the tatted doilies on the back of the sofa, all of it was in perfect order. It was almost like no one had ever come in this room, ever.

"This," I said, waving my hand around, "is where my grandfather met with visitors."

"Okay," Aaron said, like he was as sure as I was about why I had given him that information.

"I got to see . . . ," I said. Check and see if what I was feeling about things was the way they were.

We walked down the hall, our feet making whisper sounds on the wooden floor. Aaron stood close behind me. I could hear him breathing. The kitchen door was open. The sink brimmed with water. I hurried past the half bath, where that sink too, was full—to the bottom of the stairs that led up to the bedrooms and the big bathroom that Momma and Aunt Linda and I had shared over a year ago.

Neither Aaron nor I moved. Stood there. Looking up.

She's gone. She's gone. She's gone.

"Seems like all the lights are on up there, too," Aaron said. His voice was near my ear. "Does your mom usually leave everything turned on?"

Was he scared? He didn't sound it.

You are.

Yes, I was afraid. Heart-thumping terrified.

"No," I said. "Just the opposite." My hand rested on the

oak banister that wiggled a little when you touched it. I could smell the storm coming, dark and damp. "Especially in bad weather. She thinks lightning will strike us if we're using the electricity."

"Oh." Aaron glanced behind himself, like maybe he measured the distance from where we stood to the front door and freedom.

"You can go home now, if you want," I said, giving him a chance to get away.

"No," he said. "I'm staying. Till you find her."

Relief surged through me. "I better check upstairs then." I paused. And looked him right in the face. "If you're sure."

"I'm sure."

Up we went then, his words the permission we needed. The landing was spotless, but had a musty, closed-up smell. Something it took me a minute to adjust to every time I came in from outside.

At the top of the stairs, I started thinking awful stuff.

Like what if Momma had killed herself? Or had fallen in the bathroom, where I knew we'd see the tub and sink full of water. Had banged her head? Had bled to death?

Outside thunder sounded and, as if on cue, the rain started, pinging on our tin roof. I switched the landing lights off. A long square of light fell from the bathroom, stopping at our feet. Behind us, the stairs were dark, but the last bits of sunshine splashed up the steps from the living room.

"My room first," I said. I felt out of air.

Aaron said nothing, just hung close to me. I pushed open my door. Everything on in here too, even my desk lamp and the bulb in the closet.

But nothing else was changed. A deep breath of wind pushed into the room from the two open windows, blowing the curtains out till they almost touched the twin bed, still unmade, my jammies dropped on the floor where I'd stepped out of them. The closet door ajar.

I switched everything off, closed the closet with a slam, then shut the windows halfway.

"Momma's room," I whispered. "Let's check there."

Past the bathroom we tiptoed. Lights on. Tub full. Sink filled to overflowing. Momma's almost dried and dirty foot-prints, feet bare, on the pale pink tile.

"She was here," I said. Not that I had to. "But it's been a while."

"Uh-huh?" said Aaron, like it was a question.

How would I find Momma in her room? Dressed in nightclothes? Clean from a bath? Wearing Granddaddy's old flannels shirt and blue jeans that were so big she had to tie them on?

Would she be half-naked? Angry at a stranger following me? Sleeping?

I tapped at the door and waited.

There was no sound from inside the room. Only the sigh of the storm, the patter of the rain from outside.

Turning the doorknob, I held my breath. I half expected, opening Momma's bedroom door, to see her crouched in a corner in a T-shirt, her hair straggly, her eyes showing white. Here the lamp was on, too. I glanced around the room quick. But she wasn't anywhere to be seen.

"What?" Aaron said. His voice sounded surprised. "Why?"

"Why what?" I said.

Aaron sounded breathless. "Why all the stuff? Why all the food?"

"Oh." I waved my hand in the air, dismissing it. Then I looked back into my mother's room and saw it the way it must look to Aaron.

Stacked to the ceiling along one wall were tuna, peaches, green beans, and other canned foods. On the side of the room that had a window was the toilet paper. Sanitary napkins. Tampons. Pads of paper bought cheap at Shopko. Crawling up the wall, covering most of the window. Boxes and boxes of M&M's with almonds reached for the ceiling, too. And clothes, all different kinds of clothes, stored in plastic containers. Every wall, every window in the room, was hidden with Momma's storage. Food, clothing, emergency items. All the things Granddaddy had said she should buy.

I spun around, facing Aaron, feeling defensive all the sudden. I leaned in his face. "What?" I said.

He almost couldn't get the words out. "There's so much," he said.

"So?"

"I mean, it's like a grocery store in here. Why do you have it all, Lacey?"

Yes, why?

I had no answer. I looked back in the room again. At everything. So much of everything that the two windows were blocked.

"I told you," I said, turning to face Aaron. I clenched my teeth. Balled my fists. "I warned you things weren't right." I stared at him. Daring him. Daring him to run. To leave. So what! So what if I didn't have a friend. So what if I was alone. I had been alone with Momma for a year. What was one more day?

"Oh," Aaron said.

And then as fast as the defensiveness had come, a wave of tiredness swept over me. For a moment, I didn't think I could keep up the search for my mother. For a moment, I wanted to walk back down the stairs, out the door, and down the road. Away.

Where? Where? Where?

Yes, to where? There was no place to go. Not even St. Augustine.

I was here. I had to be here. In this place. Taking care of Momma. I looked Aaron in the eyes again. "She's sick," I said. "I gotta find her."

After snapping off the light, I pulled the door to Momma's room closed. My fingers trembled.

Aaron and I stood face-to-face in the darkened hall. I could feel the heat coming from him. Was he scared, too? We stood close enough I could have hugged him if I wanted. Could have held his hand if I'd had the nerve. If he didn't run.

"Let's find her," he said. His voice was light as a new leaf.

Oh. Oh. Good. Only finding Momma was important.

No bit of light stretched toward us from under Aunt Linda's door. "One more room," I said.

I hadn't been in Aunt Linda's room since she left. Not even when I missed her bad. A couple of times, I'd stood outside the door, with my ear pressed to the wood, listening for my aunt. But Momma caught me once, and yelled. Told me to stop wishing for the dead to come back. Told me things were different and could never be fixed. Would never be the same.

Then for a couple of weeks things started smelling awful

near Aunt Linda's room. It was when Momma was doing her wanderings.

"Something's dead up there I think," I told her. I was afraid. Had taken to sleeping on the sofa in the living room. "The smell's coming from Aunt Linda's room."

"It's Granddaddy," Momma said. "He's killed rats in there. And mice, too. Stay away."

So I did. I never went in that room. Never. And not because of rats and mice. I didn't go in 'cause I was sure it would hurt too much. Hurt my heart to see the room made up the way Aunt Linda kept it. Light and airy. Windows wide like in my room. So when I stood there with Aaron, it took me a moment to open the door.

But at last, I did.

The light was off. Everything in here was dark.

"Momma?" My voice went into the airless room. Dust and paper smell filled my nose.

My hand searched the wall for the light switch and I touched something crinkly. Then *snap!* The dim overhead bulb came on.

"What?" I said it this time.

My head wouldn't let me understand, wouldn't let me see things right for a moment. This wasn't Aunt Linda's room. Not anymore.

Pages from books had been stuck to the walls. All the

books Aunt Linda left. They were now on the floor in neat stacks, the covers. And thousands of words coated all the walls, millions of words maybe, hid the soft lavender-colored wallpaper that had been here before my aunt went away.

What was going on?

"Momma?" I heard my voice like someone else had said the word. I walked in the room. My legs seemed broken at the knees. On the dresser I saw it.

Mr. Dewey's cage.

And Mr. Dewey inside. Feathers now, with bones.

"Mr. Dewey." Again my voice sounded strange. Not like me. "What happened?" I stepped up to the dresser and looked at what was left of the bird. Dust covered everything. I meant to say, "No. No." But I'm not sure the words came out of my mouth at all.

In a slow circle, I turned, my eyes burning from what was in front of me. The long mirror, just words. The closet doors, just words. The walls, the windows, everything—just words.

"Who's in the bed?" Aaron's voice sounded bizarre.

I made myself look. To the body shape that was covered with an old quilt. Granddaddy's quilt.

"Momma?" Another word I meant to say. But all that came out was air.

I'm not sure how I got to the side of the bed. Not sure

how long the walk took. Not sure how long I stood there, checking for signs of breathing. And seeing none.

"Don't look," Aaron said. "Maybe we should call the police." His hand gripped my arm. Squeezing hard. Hurting. I wiggled away from him.

"Maybe it's her," I said, and my voice was full of tears.

Maybe Momma had killed herself in this room. Where I might not look. Where I might never go.

In the book-darkness of the room, my hand reached out on its own. I pulled back the covers.

Auburn hair, showed first. Hair like . . .

. . . like my aunt's.

It's her. Here all the time. Dead. Right here!

Aunt Linda?

A buzzing sound went off in my ears. It felt like there was no blood around my mouth.

"I saw her drive away," I said. I moved the blanket a little more. A bone-white forehead.

"John said she visited the library."

Aunt Linda.

Glassy eyes.

That smell.

Red lipstick.

"A mannequin," Aaron said. And his breath came out with the words, full of relief.

A wave of dizziness swept over me. But I put my head down, resting my hands on my knees, and after a moment was sure I could stand again. Where had Momma gotten a mannequin?

"Lacey?" Aaron said. "Are you okay?"

I shook my head.

No. No, I wasn't okay.

Outside the rain beat steady and hard on the roof.

I looked up at Aaron.

For a moment I wrestled with what I knew I should do. But this part of me, this part all hurt and sad, didn't want to do it.

Because my aunt had let me down. She hadn't done her part.

And now all this. All this.

She wasn't dead. Not like Mr. Dewey. There was Mr. Dewey over there. And a mannequin here. Not a human being. Not my aunt after all.

"We better call her," I said. "We better call my aunt Linda."

XI

It was easy to find Aunt Linda's phone number. All I had to do was look in my head and remember what I hadn't let myself think about in a long time.

But it wasn't as easy to *call* her.

First of all, my hands shook so much I couldn't press all those numbers. Second, she had left me. *Left* me with Momma.

I knew the logic of it all. That Momma wouldn't let Aunt Linda stay here. She chased her away. She threatened her with the police. With restraining orders.

I knew what Aunt Linda had said, about trying to get back to see me.

And I knew that I couldn't have left Momma anyway. Not alone. What would she do without me to take care of her? How would she make it?

Still, calling Aunt Linda was like I had given in or something.

We walked down the stairs to the front room. I picked up the phone, steadied it in my hands. Hoped for one moment of calm.

"You okay?" Aaron said.

I nodded. A lie.

"You need help?"

She *left* me!

"Lacey, I think we need to call someone."

I squeezed the phone. Nodded again.

Momma was gone. I *had* to do it. I *had* to call Aunt Linda. Even if she did leave. There was Mr. Dewey. And that mannequin. All those words on her bedroom walls.

"Let me dial," Aaron said at last.

I handed the phone over to him for the second time that day. Then I went and peeked out the living room window at our large yard and the houses beyond.

Where was she? Where?

It's all your fault.

The trees were dark with rain, bending a little with the wind. It was like night outside, the sky dim and clouded over.

All my fault? Yes, yes it was. If I hadn't insisted on Momma getting that job. If I hadn't wanted a moment to myself. A chance to stretch without being afraid. A chance to get out of here. None of this would have happened.

I leaned my forehead against the windowpane. It felt cool. "Momma." *I* almost couldn't hear myself. "Where are you? And what in the heck is going on here? Tell me what's happening."

I remembered a book I read by Louise Plummer. About a girl whose grandmother was missing. And was found dead under the neighbor's porch. Was that Momma's fate? Was she gone from me already? Had she hidden herself under someone else's porch to stay out of the rain?

She's dead.

I squeezed my eyes shut. No!

She wasn't! I knew it! I felt it!

Behind me I heard Aaron's voice. "Please call Lacey back." He was leaving a message.

Aunt Linda wasn't there. Funny how my heart felt like it plunged near my toes. I kept looking out into the yard. Kept staring into the rain. Fogging up the window with breath that kept me from crying.

"Does your aunt work?" Aaron asked.

I looked back at him. Standing there with the phone against his chest. "Yeah. At the library in St. Augustine."

Aaron called information. I heard him waiting. I thought of Momma missing in the storm. Walking out there lost. All afraid. Confused. There was a crash of lightning so loud I screamed. The lights we'd left on blinked out. The house fell into a muddy-water darkness.

"I'm here, Lacey," Aaron said. And then, "Linda? You don't know me. I live in Peace."

I turned in a slow circle. *Aunt Linda.*

"Lacey?" Aaron said, into the phone and to me at the same time.

Aunt Linda.

That walk across the living room seemed so long. One of the longest I've ever taken. I took the warm phone in my hand and swallowed down at the lump that grew fat in my throat. The way I'd done in school so many times. The way I'd done so many nights after my aunt left. The way I'd wanted to swallow away this past year.

Then I said, "I need you now."

My mouth grew spitty, like I'd been crying for years.

"Lacey?" Aunt Linda said.

"Yes, it's me," I said.

I couldn't think of the words.

All those words in that room.

142

"What's wrong, Lacey?"

"I can't find Momma," I said.

"I'll be there in less than twenty minutes." The phone clicked dead.

She was on her way.

AARON AND I sat in the semidarkness for a few minutes. Outside the storm hammered at us. Inside the air was heavy and hot.

"Should we open the windows?" he said.

The thought was so strange. The only windows ever opened in the house were the two in my room where I slept. And before, the ones in Aunt Linda's room.

I thought for a minute. Momma wouldn't like it much. But.

"Sure," I said. "Good idea."

Around we went, pushing at windows that squeaked out protests at being forced open. Straightaway the air outside started cleansing the air inside. Making it smell newer. Damp and clear and a little chilly.

Lightning made the trees look blue.

"The dining room and the kitchen, too," I said. "Let's get those open in there."

"Okay," Aaron said.

We made our way through the main floor, letting fresh, clean air into the house. Rain came in some of the screens.

"I'll clean it up with a towel later," I said when Aaron pointed it out.

Sadness came at me like the wind.

"My momma," I said, as we walked into the kitchen. "She thought that evil spirits could get in through the screens. So we kept things closed up."

He didn't say anything. I was glad that the lights were off. I couldn't quite make out his face. He was probably bug-eyed right about now. Evil spirits, right. But I saw him nod.

I let myself down into a chair.

Aaron sat next to me. The smell of rain rushed through the house with the wind.

"My dead granddaddy tells her that."

"Oh."

Soon as the words were out of my mouth, I knew I sounded crazy as Momma. If I'd had the energy, I would have defended Granddaddy *and* Momma. But I was worn out. So tired I was sure I'd never get up from that chair again. And, somehow, the dark made me truthful.

"He doesn't really talk to her." I took in a gulp of the storm air. It smelled so new. "I mean, I've never heard him myself."

"That's good," Aaron said. He let out a little laugh.

I wanted to laugh, too. Instead, I leaned against the table. Every part of me was heavy as bricks.

"Lacey?" Aaron said.

"She's not here," I said at last. "If Momma had been here, we'd have found her by now." I looked out the kitchen door at the rain that fell like silver to the ground. I wanted to weep.

Aaron said nothing.

"I feel like someone's squeezed the life from me. I feel like an old dishrag." I stared into the backyard. Watched the rain. "I'm worried I'll never see her again. Maybe she got hit by a car. I never even thought of calling the hospital." Fear and grief, like fists, clutched at my insides.

"She didn't get hit by a car," Aaron said. "We would have seen the ambulance. Heard the sirens. Something. And anyway. She's been here. You know that. We saw all the water. All the lights. She's okay, Lacey."

Outside the rain lessened a bit. The storm was moving on some. Not sitting right over the house.

"And what about Aunt Linda? Why isn't she here yet?" I said. "St. Augustine isn't that far."

"It's only been a couple of minutes since we called her," Aaron said. "The storm'll slow her down some."

He was right.

"Thank you." I paused.

Aaron shrugged. "No big deal."

What if Aaron hadn't spoken to me on the bus? What if he hadn't said he would come back with me? I'da come here alone. Again. Found things this way. I moved near him. Kept my voice soft, almost a whisper. "I'm not so sure I coulda done it by myself. You know." With my head I gestured at the ceiling even though I knew he couldn't quite see me. I thought of this miracle. How Aaron was here at just this time. Aunt Linda would say Aaron was a gift. "It's all so freaky. I'm not so sure what would have happened."

Remembering my aunt's room sent a shiver through me. And Mr. Dewey, dead. What would John think? What would Aunt Linda do? I shivered again. Had a goose run across my grave? Something Momma said when she saw me tremble for no reason.

"I don't have a grave," I had told her once.

"But you will," she had said back.

"You would have done it, Lacey," Aaron said. In the darkness of the room I could just see the blond of his hair. Could see his lips moving. There was a slim bit of light coming from somewhere outside. Light a person could talk in.

"You would have been fine if I hadn't been here."

"I don't know," I said again. "I've never been this afraid before." That was true. I had seen Momma do some scary stuff. But not like this.

The room's been like that a long time. And Mr. Dewey too, in there a long time.

I closed my eyes to the voice. Opened them to glance at Aaron.

That was true, too. The pages on Aunt Linda's wall. That little bird dead. Maybe even the mannequin was something that had been there in that room for who knows how long. Just because I didn't know what was behind a closed door didn't mean it hadn't been there.

"I've never been this worried for her." Aaron said nothing. "I've always found her."

I didn't know how to explain what sat in my gut. A fear that something awful, something *awful,* had happened.

All of the things Momma had done didn't amount to the way I felt. Somehow the bits and pieces were easier to clean up after. But this—how was I to clean up after something I couldn't even see to fix?

"I've always found her before," I said again. "And before that, Aunt Linda was here."

It was then that Aaron took my hand. Just reached over and held my hand like it was something he did every day.

"Lacey," he said. "You got guts. You've done things here no one at school could even begin to take care of."

You do what you have to do. It was Momma's voice in my head.

You make it because you have to.

You crawl through whatever crap is thrown at you.

All my mother's words of wisdom. Sitting there in my head.

I didn't want them a moment longer.

But they're here.

So I'd get rid of them. I would.

'Cause truth be told, I wouldn't want to do any more of this kind of stuff with her. Not any more of it.

I wanted a mother who was happy, and an aunt who never left. I didn't want to tend my momma's self-inflicted wounds. Didn't want to make all her meals and clean her clothes and stay up with her at night watching for someone who'd been dead more than a decade.

Aaron called his mother after a while. Then he came back and sat down again. "She said she'd pick me up in a few minutes." He gave a shrug, like maybe that's how mothers were. "She doesn't want me skateboarding home in the rain."

I nodded.

"I told her to give me some time to wait for your aunt here."

He sat next to me at the kitchen table close enough that our forearms touched. We both looked to the back door, to the rain, the whole house waiting behind us, like it was alive. I felt his skin on mine, felt the house breathing, felt worry and confusion and a little bit of happiness pushing in on the grief.

"Once," I said, the memory fresh in my mind with the rain, "when Aunt Linda was still here, we found Momma outside during a storm like this."

Aaron said nothing, moved a little in his seat. Looked me in the face.

I gestured with my head. "She was out there, standing, arms raised to the sky."

I could see it all in my head again, the way she looked like an old picture, black and white in the darkness and downpour. I left out the part that Momma was naked. That it was winter and near to freezing.

"Her hair was plastered to her face and her eyes were like shadowed circles in her head. When Aunt Linda tried to get her in the house, she fought."

The fight hadn't lasted long, Momma was too weak to do much. Too cold. But slippery like a just-caught fish. Aunt Linda dragged her into the kitchen where I waited with a housecoat for Momma and towels for them both.

Aunt Linda had Momma sit where I sat now. I knelt at Momma's feet and dried off her legs where dead leaves and dirt had splattered. Her big toe was bleeding, the nail almost torn off.

"Let me make you some tea," Aunt Linda had said, and she put water in the kettle to boil.

Momma never said a thing. Just shivered with the cold. Her arms and legs so thin. Her hair dripping. Her eyes a blank. And when the water boiled and the kettle whistled, Momma looked down at me. She put her hands on my head.

Right at that moment, when I looked into her face, I saw my old mother, from a long time ago. It was like I looked at her real self, trapped somewhere behind her eyes.

"Lacey," she said, her hands on my cheeks, gentle near my ears. "Lacey, I love you."

The memory made my insides turn around. Made tears come. But I wasn't about to let them fall.

"What happened then?" Aaron said.

I shrugged. I couldn't go on. "She was fine," I said at last.

But looking back I knew it wasn't true. Things hadn't been fine in this house for a long, long time. Except for that one moment when my real momma looked out at me.

"Are you sure it's okay for me to go?" Aaron said after lightning lit the sky so that I could see his face clearly. "Are you sure you don't want me to hang around a little longer? You know, till your aunt gets here?"

I shook my head no. Thinking of Momma afraid and in the dark and wet made me want to bawl my face off. And if I was going to cry, I wanted to do it alone.

Aaron stood, and I did, too. We walked through the house to the front door. *Don't cry,* I thought. *Whatever you do, don't cry. Not now.*

"Everything's going to be okay," I said. I could hear my voice going tight and high, like I was a balloon full of helium. "As soon as Aunt Linda pulls in the driveway, I'll be fine. She'll know what to do." *She'll know where Momma's gone.* "And she should be here any second now, right? Probably before *your* momma even."

Aaron must not have been able to tell how close I was to bawling. He smiled. We stood together in the hall, shoulders touching, our skin damp from the humidity, watching out the front door for his momma or my aunt. With me ignoring as many tears as the rain had cried during this storm.

You did it! You lost her!

I didn't! I didn't.

I remembered Aunt Linda, her voice smooth after a time when Momma had cried over something she saw on the news. First she'd tucked Momma into bed. And then to me she said, "She'll be fine, Lacey. If we keep her on her meds, she'll be fine."

But that hadn't happened.

Momma refused anything that she had to swallow whole. She said the government put something in the medicine to record people's thoughts.

That memory seemed to suck out all my courage now. I wanted to just fall on the floor in a clump. And when Aunt Linda got home, I planned on letting her take care of everything.

Now I was *ready* for Aaron to go. I just felt too sad. I needed crying time before my aunt got home.

Cars drove past, splashing water in waves from the puddles in the street. Everything was pure dark. I could see the power was off everywhere. No houses showed lights. The lightning was less harsh and further away.

A car came up the road, driving slowly through the rain and puddles.

"There she is," Aaron said. "My mom."

"Oh, that's good," I said.

I was struck with a deep jealousy seeing that car. In my whole life I couldn't remember Momma ever coming and getting me from anywhere. No matter the weather. Or dropping me off anywhere either, for that matter. She used to go out of the house just to shop for food, before the money ran out. That's why I'd thought a job at the Winn-Dixie would be a good thing. That's why I had encouraged her to look for work there. I had thought, somehow, being around all that food would make her feel comfortable.

Aaron and I stepped onto the front porch that was slick with rain. He picked up his skateboard as his mother pulled into our driveway. The headlights lit up the side of my house, made the dark seem even darker.

"Thanks again," I said.

"Sure," he said. Then all the sudden he was in my face and his lips were on the corner of my mouth, catching mostly my cheek. There just a second. Soft and warm.

And me not even expecting it.

I touched the place he'd kissed.

"I'll come over and we'll do some skateboarding," he said. Then he splashed through the soppy front yard. He waved again at the car, calling out, "You're going to find her soon. I know it." Then I watched him drive away until even the red of the taillights was gone for good.

XII

I stood on the front porch. Everything was so weird. Me calling Aunt Linda. Momma being gone so long. Aaron kissing me. And my tears. With Aaron gone, you'da thunk I could have cried enough to make a yard soppy myself.

But no. I stood dry-eyed there in the front of my house. Darkness everywhere. Thunder sounding in the distance. The rain splashing in puddles. Worried about Momma, surprised at Aaron, waiting for Aunt Linda.

A breeze ran through the yard. I heard the palm fronds scratching at the wind. And like that, a mist of warm rain, almost like a low cloud, fell from the black sky. I leaned against Granddaddy's ancient Adirondack chair. It left a thin line of water on my thigh. From somewhere came the soft scent of roses.

A car drove past, lights like eyeballs cutting into the darkness. When would Aunt Linda come?

My whole body seemed to churn at the worries, my tummy dropping away from me with the thoughts, like when you take on the Zipper ride at the fair.

Then that anger was back again, surprising me.

If Momma hadn't gone away, then this whole day would have been different. If Momma hadn't left this would have been a promise fulfilled. Corny, but true.

"If you hadn't run off, I wouldn't be standing outside. If...," my mind started heading places I didn't let it go, "...if you were different, this wouldn't have happened. If you woulda gone for help."

I paused. Who was I to talk to Momma like this?

Who are you?

Stop! Don't even think that!

I knew who I was. Someone mad. Really bent out of shape.

I *deserved* to speak my mind, even if it was to my own self.

"If you were a real momma," I said, clenching my fists, "you'd be taking care of me."

Aunt Linda wouldn't have been forced to leave.

Mr. Dewey would be singing at the library.

I might have friends.

Guilt and loneliness and confusion filled me. It seemed to crawl right up my lungs and into my mouth. Why should I have to feel any of these things? It wasn't fair.

"Don't think this way," I said.

And then, "Yes, do."

I took in a deep breath.

"Get it together, Lacey. Do what you have to." I imagined Aunt Linda home. To stay. But she wasn't here yet. I looked down the street again.

Think straight.

Right.

Momma, I knew, was in trouble. Big trouble. I could see that when I looked at my world through Aaron's eyes. All the food stored up in the bedroom. The closed windows. The running off. All that water. The mannequin. The words taped everywhere.

And Mr. Dewey. Poor Mr. Dewey. These last things seemed weird even to me. I felt angry with Momma. Gypped.

And there was the sorrow.

I stood outside waiting for Aunt Linda a few more minutes.

The rain became smaller, more innocent drops, but I still didn't go inside. Gusts of wind pushed the mist at me, wetting my face, cooling me, almost calming me.

"Everything," I said to the dark night sky, "everything is going to be okay. I'm going to just forget it all. Like none of it has ever happened."

I started back into the house. The screen door opened with a squeak. Careful not to make too much noise, I let it close with a small wooden *fump*.

Coming inside frightened me a little. Sure, I'd been plenty scared at home before. Momma and her weird self. The way she'd be sometimes at night when she'd keep me awake. Us lying in her bed together. Her arms around me tight from her fear. Her hot breath at the back of my neck.

"Don't close your eyes, Lacey. Don't close them. If they're always open the aliens can't get you."

Somehow Momma had known whenever I drifted to sleep. She poked me awake. "They put things in your brain. Strips of metal. They torture you. But not if you stay alert. You can fight 'em off if you're alert. I have. I've kept them away."

Now I checked out the dirty screen toward the night sky heavy with dark clouds. No aliens.

Checked out the road. No Aunt Linda, either.

My skin was damp and so were my clothes. I glanced at the clock. Only twenty-five minutes had passed since we called Aunt Linda.

Thoughts of Momma and her talk kept coming.

"Granddaddy didn't want to die," she would sometimes say when she couldn't get out of bed for sadness's sake. "Using the choke chain?—why that was purely accidental."

I would say, "Yes, Momma."

And she would say, "That I found him? He wanted that. 'Cause we'd been so close for so long. That's why he visits me and no one else."

"Yes, Momma."

Standing there in the living room now, I squeezed my hands.

"Aaron," I whispered. Not so sure why. He seemed like the only normal thing I knew. And I wanted something, *anything,* normal. Anything. I let my hands relax and then closed my eyes. Rolled my head back, trying to ease the knots in my neck.

I kept my eyes closed as long as I could, taking deep cleansing breaths, then let them open slow like.

That's when I saw him.

At first I wasn't sure I saw anything at all. So I blinked like people on TV do. You know, a bunch of times, trying to understand. Trying to clear my head.

But no. There he was.

Granddaddy.

I drew in a breath so hard it hurt my lungs. Made my nose burn. From the back of the house, I could hear the thumping of the wind coming through the door. Could smell rain.

I stared. All I could see was the paleness of his skin. The dark splotches where eyes had been. Him draped in white. He paused on the step, turned and looked right at me. Then floated up the stairs.

I quit breathing. Not even a scream would come.

All along he had been here.

Momma *hadn't* imagined Granddaddy.

After a second, a noise came from upstairs. The *click* of a door opening. The sound of it shutting.

I couldn't walk. I tried to, but fell to one knee, hitting hard on the wooden floor.

"Aunt Linda? Where are you? Come quick." That's what I tried to say. But only a moan escaped from me.

Where to go? Where to go? Tears leaked down my cheeks. My nose turned snuffy. Far away thunder sounded. Still no lights.

"He's real. He's here."

Back from the dead. In my head I heard Momma's words. Heard her fighting with Aunt Linda that last evening.

"I seen him. Daddy visits me. Almost every night. Sometimes when you're at work. Sometimes when you're sleeping in the next room."

"No he doesn't, Angela. He doesn't."

"I tell you, Linda," Momma's voice was a spray of words, "our daddy talks to me. Tells me things. And he'd talk to you too, if you gave him a chance."

I had peered out my door, listening to them fight. Crouched near the ground so they wouldn't find me.

"He's told me the end's coming."

"Angela." Aunt Linda's voice, so sad.

"Told me that birds carry diseases. Not to eat chicken. Fish only."

"He's . . . ," Aunt Linda's voice was slow and tired, ". . . dead. You found him yourself in your bedroom, hanging in the closet."

"I remember that," Momma said, her voice angry, the words sharp like razors. "*I* pulled him down. *I* tried to revive him. *I* called for help."

"Daddy," Aunt Linda said, "is gone, Angela. It's time for you to get help. Time for you to let him go."

There was a pause then and for a moment I had thought

maybe they were done. That the fight was over. That I could go to bed. Not worry about them.

Then Momma: "You are jealous, Linda. You want to see him again and you're jealous that he visits me only."

"Oh Angela," Aunt Linda had said. "Oh Angela." She started crying. From my hiding place I watched her slump to the floor. Put her face in her hands.

Now in the downstairs hallway, with my heart trying to get away from me, I realized my mother was right. Had been all along. Granddaddy *was* here. Warning Momma. Trying to keep us safe. Telling Momma the things to do.

It was true.

I had seen him myself.

XIII

When I could move, when I could breathe, I made my way into the living room and sat down. My head spun. I thought I might pass out. But I couldn't let that happen.

I needed to be awake if Granddaddy came back.

The thought made me wanna puke. Talking to a dead man. It scared the crap outta me. But if anyone knew where Momma was, he did. Dead people know everything, right? And if she was . . . if she was dead herself, he'd know it.

Please, I thought. *Please don't let her be dead.*

Tears came to my eyes again. If Momma was gone—really gone—I didn't think I could bear it at all. I'd been so angry with her. Had wanted to get rid of her.

I sat on the sofa that Momma and I had watched the news on. I remembered her arm, soft, around me. The way she cuddled me to her as she cried because of some world injustice. Me crying with her every once in a while because her sadness was contagious, like the flu.

"Momma," I whispered now. "Momma. Where are you?"

I rested my head in my hands. Except for the ghost, I was alone.

No Momma. No aunt. Not even Aaron.

Just my dead grandfather. The thought made my skin buzz like the lightning was too close.

I'm not sure when it came to me that I needed to go looking for him. Wrestled with the thought some. But at last, I knew it.

Momma was lost. I had to find her. Aunt Linda, it seemed, wasn't coming.

But Granddaddy, as a ghost, must know everything. I'd seen him go up the stairs. And not come back down. Maybe he flew out the window or something. Or maybe he was still up there, waiting. Maybe he had a message. A message for me. From Momma, maybe.

"That's it," I said. "That's gotta be it."

The more I thought about it, the more I knew he was probably sitting on Momma's bed, waiting. All I had to do was stand, walk up the stairs, open Momma's bedroom door, and talk to him.

"But there are no lights," I said. "I'm not so sure I can meet a ghost with no lights burning. I don't want to do this." My hands shook.

Of course, there was a flashlight. Momma had a store of them and batteries in the kitchen cupboard.

"A test," I said. Even though I whispered, my voice seemed loud in the house. "If I can make it into the kitchen alone, I can make it up the stairs."

But I wasn't so sure. When I stood up, my legs were so wobbly they almost couldn't hold my weight. My body was so covered in goose bumps that my damp clothes hurt. In baby steps, I started down the hall. Sounds like the ocean pounded in my ears.

"Into the kitchen. Into the kitchen. You just have to make it into the kitchen."

There was very little light. Outside the clouds hid the slender moon. From far away came the rumble of thunder. The wind still moved the trees with a swishing noise. I could hear it in the hall. Could see the movement through the screen door that seemed to stay far away, even though I walked closer and closer.

"I'm in a dream," I said, "a nightmare," and remembered the mice with nails that cut.

That dream had been an omen. An omen of bad things to come.

In the kitchen I had to sit down again before I got the batteries from the cabinet and the flashlight from the drawer. My hands shook. My legs shook. Even my breathing was shaky.

"Aunt Linda," I said, when I at last had the energy to get back to my feet, "can't you get here?"

But though I waited for a moment, I didn't hear her car in the drive.

Do it yourself. You gotta do it yourself.

So, at last, I did.

Got the batteries in the flashlight. Flicked it on.

A stream of light so bright it almost hurt slashed through the kitchen.

"Okay, now. Okay."

For a moment the brightness seemed to help. Seemed to draw me along behind it as I pointed the way back down the hall. But when I got to the stairs, things appeared more eerie. More dark around the light.

"You can do it," I said. "Follow the light. For Momma."

Up the stairs, slow. One-at-a-time slow.

The pictures, hanging on the walls, caught the beam and shone like little mirrors. I stopped and looked at the photo of Momma and Granddaddy, standing together.

I had to keep going. "Can't wait here all night staring at a picture," I said. "Gotta find him. Gotta find Granddaddy." I made my voice a little singsongy. "Go toward the light."

Wasn't as funny as I thought it might be. My voice came out wispy.

One step at a time. One step at a time. Up I went. So scared I could hardly make my legs move. The shaft of light trembled. I smelled dust from the floor above. I was getting closer. Getting closer to a place I did not want to be. Getting closer to a place I *had* to be on account of my momma being gone. And my dead grandfather being here.

"It's just not fair," I said. "I don't want to do this."

Ahead of me, up at the top of the dark stairs came a swishing, rustling sound.

It was at that point I had to stop and gasp in a big breath. I felt tears drop out of my eyes.

The door to one of the bedrooms clicked shut.

"Granddaddy."

Keep going, I thought. *If anyone knows where Momma is, it's Granddaddy. He won't hurt you. Dead things can't hurt you.*

But I wasn't so sure of that. Thoughts of Momma cutting

herself with a razor blade popped into my head. Me finding her squatting in the bathtub. Her watching the blood splat out on the enamel like thin, red quarters. Me asking why. Momma saying, "Granddaddy told me to. Keeps us safe." Momma looking at me. "Keeps you and me safe." Aunt Linda gone. Me making Momma drop the blade. Squeezing her wrist. Squeezing it hard so she'd drop the razor. Then bandaging up the wounds.

A wave of nausea swept through me. I doubled over and held my stomach, willing myself to breathe in deep. The ray of the flashlight glowed on my foot.

"It'll be okay," I said to my toes. Even if Granddaddy told me something bizarre, it didn't mean I had to do it.

"All I need," I said, before straightening up, "all I need is information."

He could give me that, and then I'd be outta there and looking for Momma.

XIV

If Granddaddy had been a nice ghost, you'da thunk he'd come out to meet me. Not forced me to get up to the second floor to search. But he was as nice as Momma made him out to be. He left me standing on the stairs till my courage filled up and I could walk.

Ahead of me, the hall between all the bedrooms seemed like a place I'd never been before.

"Good feelings. Good feelings," I said. "Remember good times."

Like Aaron.

I could smile because of Aaron.

And other good times. Good family times.

There were some. Aunt Linda and Momma and me, all up here in our jammies, playing hide-and-seek. All of us laughing so hard I wet my pants, and then the two of them laughing even harder.

Me waking up in the middle of night for no reason. Waking the two of them.

"Warm milk," Momma would say.

"Cookies," Aunt Linda would say.

And the three of us would come downstairs and eat a meal if we wanted, until we were stuffed and happy, then go back to our separate rooms and sleep until late in the morning. Even if it meant I missed a day of school.

The times before Aunt Linda left, when Momma and me and her made a tent in one of our rooms and told ghost stories.

Now, as scary as those nights had been—and I had done plenty of shaking and screaming and laughing—they seemed like nothing compared to this whole day.

At last I stood in the hall. The bedroom doors all shut. Only the bathroom was open. With an unsteady hand I shined the flashlight toward that room. No ghost that I could see. But the sink and tub and toilet looked strange and white.

It was while I looked at the tub that I realized Granddaddy wasn't in Momma's room. Why would he wait for me there? I knew, standing so weak-kneed, that he was in *my* room. If I wanted to talk to him at all, I had to go in my own room to do it, the place where he died.

"Go now," I said, my voice coming out old and crinkled like thrown-away newspaper. "Go now for Momma."

I took a step forward. "I can't." Kept walking somehow. Put my hand on the antique doorknob. So cold under my sweaty hand. Turned. Opened the door with a little push.

"Granddaddy?"

Heavenly Father? Momma didn't believe in God. Only in ghosts. But Aunt Linda taught me to pray.

Heavenly Father. Help me. I don't think I can do this.

I stood in my doorway. I made the flashlight beam trace over my room. Each thing. The lamp. My desk. Books. All around the room. Without meaning to, I gagged. I had to take deep breaths to keep from puking.

Unmade bed. Closet door opened a bit. The flashlight beam spilling onto the floor. Dresser with a jewelry box on it.

Nothing. No ghost. No Granddaddy.

But I had seen him

I had heard him.

He was up here. I knew. I just had to find him. And say . . .

And say what? *She's gone. Do you know where Momma is? Your oldest daughter? She ran off today?*

"Look somewhere else, Lacey." I spoke aloud, trying to make myself braver. It reminded me of a time Momma and I had come in late from somewhere. She had been terrified of a serial rapist who was hiding out in Florida. Way south of us. She thought maybe he was in the house even though we'd used a key to get in the front door.

"Follow my lead," she had whispered into the side of my head as we stepped inside that day. And in a loud voice she had called out to me, "Lacey. You got the Dobermans?"

"Huh?" I had said.

Momma gave me a big wink. "The Dobermans? Our killer dogs."

I got it! "Sure do, Momma. All three of them. And they haven't been fed today."

"Tear a man from limb to limb," Momma said.

"Yes they can."

Through the whole house we went, saying that kind of stuff. But there had been no one here then and we had ended up laughing.

Talking out loud might help me now. "Look in another room. Take your time. You don't need a Doberman tonight. Just your momma."

The scariest part was turning around. I kept expecting that horrible white face—with no eyes—to pop out at me.

I talked myself down the hall past Momma's room. *Deep cleansing breath.*

Momma was always telling me that.

"Deep cleansing breath, baby. If you're scared at school or on the bus or when you run errands for me, you just take a deep breath. It'll help get all the evil out of your body. You'll be able to think more clear."

Through my dried out lips I sucked in dusty air.

Bam!

Behind me my bedroom door slammed shut.

The scream that came out of me, I know could have been heard down to the library. I stumbled forward, hitting into Momma's door, trying to get away.

"Help me." My voice was shrill. "I can't do this alone."

And then . . .

"Help me."

My words, but not from me.

A deep, low voice.

Granddaddy's voice.

My dead grandfather.

The words from Aunt Linda's room.

173

"I can't do this alone," he said, repeating me. "You need to help me."

"Momma? Where are you? Help me," I said, my voice soft. Again I forced myself to move. I took a step toward Aunt Linda's door. Took a step toward my dead grandfather.

"Momma," he said. "Help me. I can't do it alone." Such a rumbling voice.

"Aunt Linda." I cried so hard now I shook. My whole body shook.

"Linda. Linda. Linda," said Granddaddy.

I took another step. Now all I had to do was reach out. Touch the knob. Turn it.

And Granddaddy would be there. Could tell me where Momma was.

"Do you know," I said, "where she is?"

"Do you know? Linda. Linda. Linda." A voice like gravel.

Step. Reach out. Hand on the knob. Slippery with sweat. Turning. Turning. "Granddaddy?" I said. "Where's my momma? I lost her today."

Tears all over my face. My nose running. My hands sweating. The flashlight leading the way.

Door open.

"I can't do it alone, Linda," came the voice. "Help me."

Into the room went the light. And I followed it to find my grandfather.

XV

The whole room looked fake in the flashlight beam. Like something from a movie. Not real. Books torn up and everywhere.

But it *was* real. And happening to me.

"Granddaddy?" My voice trembled, like my words were afraid to leave the safety of my mouth.

"Granddaddy." This came from the other side of the room.

I swung the flashlight toward the sound.

Nothing but words taped to the wall. So many words.

I took a step into Aunt Linda's bedroom. I thought I might puke.

"I'm here about Angela," I said. My voice sounded scared to my own ears. And old like the pages taped up in this room.

"Angela's gone."

I turned the flashlight again, twisting around to see where the voice came from. My heart pounded so hard it hurt.

"I know," I said. My tears had stopped. Somebody watching might not think I was scared beyond anything I had ever been in my life. But my hands—they gave me away. I clenched the flashlight with both, like maybe I held on to a rope that would pull me from this darkness if I was careful. The beam of light shook like crazy, bouncing around like the little dot on kids' videos showing which word should be sung in a song. "I know she's gone, Granddaddy. I gotta find her. She's alone."

I half expected Granddaddy to step out of Aunt Linda's clothes closet. Walk through the door or something. Come out and help me find his missing daughter.

But nothing happened.

I moved the beam along, lighting circles of words. Past the covered window. Over the closet doors. Toward the dresser where drawers were taped shut with more words. To the bed.

It was hard to look there. That mannequin frightened me something awful. I didn't want to see it again. It had looked so much like a dead Aunt Linda that I was still afraid to let the light rest there.

But I did. The glow showed the shape of the mannequin.

And another shape. One that moved, just a little. Covered completely.

It felt like someone had kicked all my breath away. My mouth opened and at that moment the second shape began to rise.

Then all I heard was me screaming. I took a step backward and hit the dresser. I dropped the flashlight. It bounced twice, throwing light around the room in a funny arc. Then it went out.

The room was black.

Rustling sounds came from the bed.

I dropped to my knees, onto the wool rug. Felt along for the flashlight. Tried to breathe at the same time. Couldn't seem to take in air.

Where is it? Where is that flashlight?

Inside me I could feel another scream growing. Like a wave on the beach. Getting bigger. And bigger.

Now I heard footsteps. Light like someone walking on tiptoe. I hadn't realized that ghosts touched the ground when they walk. *Where is that flashlight?* My hands felt around. Frantic. *Got to find that. Got to. Oh, help me.*

My breath came in gasps. My nose stuffed up from early tears. Hands out. Fingers reaching. Touching. Something warm. Alive.

Or dead as a ghost.

I threw myself backward with a holler. Crashed into the dresser.

"Momma!" My cry was louder than anything I had ever screamed before. It tore out of me.

"She's gone," Granddaddy said.

"No!" I scrambled around. Trying to get away. Out of the room. Away from dead people. Away from here. And at last found the flashlight. Pressed the button. *Snap*, it came on. Lit up the carpet showing old roses.

I swung the light around. Aiming right at Granddaddy's face.

"Where is my mother?" It was a scream.

He turned from the light.

Ghosts don't do that, do they?

Reached down for me.

Getting close enough for me to see.

Momma in my memory. "Daddy and me almost looked like twins. Same black eyes. Same dark hair."

"Momma? Is that you?"

Her hands out. Taking hold of my arms. Shaking. Pinching. Hurting.

"Momma?"

"She's gone."

But this was my momma. Now that I was so close, I could see that it really *was* her. I could see her soft skin. See the dark circles under her eyes. The deep scratches on her cheeks. Blood dried on her shirt and on her neck.

Relief ran through my body so fast it felt like I'd fallen into a cold winter ocean, then into something hot. Momma right here. Right in front of me. Holding on to my arms. Talking crazy but here.

"Oh thank goodness. I looked for you all day," I said. "Looked for you all over the Winn-Dixie."

Momma's hands loosened some. "Too much," she said. "Too many people for her. I took her away."

Momma talking like a man. Like Granddaddy?

"Momma?"

"I told her," Momma said. "Hanging's not a bad way to go. You kick some. Try to get free. Try to breathe. But being dead leaves everyone else with the trouble."

"Momma?" I leaned next to her. She smelled sour. Bad. Still I came close, putting my face near to hers. "It's me, Lacey."

"I see you, baby," Momma said. Her voice soft and normal. Hers again. Tired. "Granddaddy wants me to go with him. He came to get me. But I said I had to wait for you. So we could all go together."

Excuse me?

I felt like my heart changed places with my stomach.

Momma put her arms around me, tight. "We waited for you, baby. So you could come along. I didn't want you to have to do it alone. Didn't want you to find me."

"What are you talking about?" I squirmed in Momma's hold. Loosening her grip a little.

"The hardest day of my life was getting your granddaddy down," Momma said. Now her voice was sad sounding with her terrible memory. She got a better hold on me. "I didn't want you to have to do that. Didn't want you to have to breathe into my mouth. All cold." Momma tried to get us to her feet, but I sat heavy so she couldn't pull me up. She kept grabbing under my arms, like you might lift a baby. "Now that you're here, you and me can go together."

"Go where?" I said, but Momma didn't answer. She just kept pulling to get me to my feet.

With a jerk I pushed her away. "What are you telling

me?" Underneath my fingers I could feel the itchiness of the carpet.

"We'll do it in your room. Like Granddaddy did."

"We'll do what? What are you saying, Momma?"

"I found him in my closet."

"I know."

"Hanging in that closet that's yours now."

"I know."

"We'll join Granddaddy. It'll make life so much easier."

Was Momma saying I should . . . was Momma saying I should kill myself? That we kill ourselves together? Hang ourselves like my grandfather had so many years ago?

I tried to get to my feet.

"No!" My voice came out loud. Harsher than I meant. "No!"

"Lacey." The Granddaddy voice was back. "I want you both with me."

"I'm not doing it!" I scrambled away from Momma, kicking the air and the floor with my feet.

Momma grabbed me again, and this time she had such a grip that I knew a bruise formed under her fingers.

"Ouch. Momma, let me go. You're hurting me."

"Get into your room."

It was like with Granddaddy's voice came a man's

strength. I couldn't break away from my mother. So instead, I stood. And walked with Momma without a fight.

"Lookit, Momma," I said. "I'm not doing what you think Granddaddy told you to do. Whatever it is. I'm not going to do it."

"This is for the best," Momma said in that weird voice. "We'll be together. I've missed you both."

"Momma?" I squirmed a little. We walked into the dark hall, passing the stairs. "I never even knew Granddaddy. He couldn't miss me. Let me go."

Across the hall. To my closed door.

"Open it."

I did.

New air rushed out of the room. Everything felt damp and fresh in here. The moon let in light through both my windows.

"To the closet now." Momma's voice was back. She rubbed at my arms with her cool hands, like maybe she wanted to take away the pain that had been there.

"Listen," I said, turning to face her. "This isn't what I want to do." I put my arms around her and rested my head on her shoulder. "I don't want to go away. And I don't want you to, either."

"I know. But it has to be, Lacey. I won't do it without you." Momma's voice was smooth and, for the first time in a long time, she sounded determined. "I found him hanging from the rafter in my closet," she said. "It was just before you were born. I was eight months pregnant with you and so big. I almost couldn't get him down. I kept screaming for someone to call 911. But Linda was in the backyard. She didn't hear me at first."

"Don't think about that," I said. I hugged my mother tight. Tried to soothe her away from this memory.

"By the time the police did get here, Granddaddy was too dead to be helped. I kept breathing for him though. And they pulled me away. Took me to the hospital."

"And you were born that day."

I knew Granddaddy and I shared the same day, but I hadn't known what happened that afternoon. My voice came out shaky and weak, like an old man walks. "It's okay. You're all right now. I'm here," I whispered in her ear. Pet her face. Smoothed her hair.

"No, I'm not." Momma sounded weepy. "No, I'm not okay. And I don't want you to ever feel this way. It's awful. I hate the way I feel." She folded in on herself like her feelings hurt her. Then she straightened and pushed me to my closet.

"No, Momma," I said.

She pulled on the door and I turned to look behind me. A fat flashlight lit the space. There were two nooses in there. My clothes had been pushed aside, some dumped to the floor. Both ropes hung from the rafter of Momma's old closet. *My* closet. *Mine!*

"No," I screamed. "I'm not doing it." A flowerlike smell swooshed into my room with the wind. The door slammed shut.

"This is where I found him," Momma said. "We'll do it together." And then the Granddaddy voice. "Do it, Lacey."

"I won't."

"Do it."

"No!" I screamed.

The door to my room swung open, against the wind. *More ghosts,* I thought. *I can't fight any more than this.*

"Lacey? Angela? I'm here." Aunt Linda's voice.

Just a shadow of her in the darkness. But there she was. Real and in my doorway, my Aunt Linda, back home again.

XVI

Aunt Linda made me wait in the living room for the police. I was almost glad to go, seeing Momma crumple up at the sight of her sister. The dark all around them, except for that old flashlight—Granddaddy's old light—that Momma had saved all this time.

Then there was Aunt Linda pulling Momma onto her lap, like she wasn't the baby in the family, but the older, stronger sister.

I went down the stairs, hanging on to the rail like it led to salvation.

Inside I was a storm of confusion. Like, how was Aunt Linda able to calm my momma down, but not me? And why hadn't Aunt Linda just stuck around, living closer? Why couldn't she have seen what Momma and me needed?

I stood near the front door, waiting, wondering. My knees shaking something awful. My stomach just *sick*. All those whys. So many whys.

Like why Momma wanted me to die.

At last I saw the police drive up to our house, from where I peeked out past the frilly curtains. Saw the flashing lights on their cars, their guns, their faces that seemed to change from red to blue to gray in less than seconds.

"It's going to be all right," Aunt Linda had said, before I came downstairs. She put her warm hands on my shoulders. "This is the way it has to be. Your momma's worse than I imagined she could be."

"I know that," I said. "She wanted to kill me." My voice was ragged and harsh. I shrugged her hands away. Anger filled me up. "I *know* she's bad off."

Now the policemen were on the porch. I could hear their heavy shoes. And I knew Momma could, too. Hidden back in my room. Afraid. The two of them upstairs together with Granddaddy's ghost.

A policeman knocked. The sound seemed loud and

empty. I moved to open the door. Upstairs I heard a scuttling sound. Momma maybe?

"You shouldn't have gone," I had said to Aunt Linda. I stood, staring down at the two of them. Momma all wrapped up in Aunt Linda's arms. And that rope right there. "Never."

In the darkness I saw Aunt Linda look up at me, her eyes wide, her face pale as the thin moon. Behind her the old flashlight burned, making my flashlight beam puny.

"I been doing this alone. All alone, all along." Something close to pain and the feeling of being completely by myself filled me from toes to my hair's roots.

"I know it," Aunt Linda said. "I didn't want to go. I just . . ."

"You left me to do it all single-handed. You took the easy way out." I was so angry I could have spit flaming arrows. "It was hard the whole time."

"I'm sorry, Lacey," she had said. Her voice was a soft wail. "I'm so sorry. Honest to God, I'm sorry. I tried to see you. But she wouldn't let me. And a few times I even came and checked on you when I knew you were home, hoping she'd be gone."

"You didn't have to go," I said, my voice rising.

"I didn't know what else to do."

"Granddaddy's been watching over us, Linda," Momma said, soft as a pat. "Hasn't he, Lacey?"

"Yeah, right," I had said, then come down the stairs to wait.

Someone knocked again.

Weird how I couldn't quite open the door.

Another knock sounded and one of the officers called, "Anyone home?"

My hand reached for the knob. I pulled back the curtains and glanced out at the men in raincoats, their hats protected by plastic.

"Did you call for help?" One of the policemen shined his flashlight in the house through the glass and I raised my hand to shield my eyes from the brightness. "Are you alone?"

I shook my head no and opened the door. "It'll be okay," I said.

Another patrol car pulled up, then an ambulance. All those lights flashing.

"Momma and Aunt Linda are upstairs," I said. And I moved to let them inside.

MOMMA FOUGHT LIKE a wildcat. I heard it all. Once I tried to get up and see what was happening, but the ambulance lady wouldn't let me. So I sat in the living room and

listened. Listened to the crashing of furniture, to the breaking of glass things, and to my momma's screams.

Outside, the neighbors stood on their own porches.
Stood in the street. A few even braved coming into our yard.
I looked for Aaron, but I didn't see him, and I was glad for
that, at least. A part of me wanted to yell to the watchers,
"Get away." But I didn't. Momma and me didn't share anything with our neighbors before. There was no need for me
to share anything more than what they would see tonight.

Things calmed down at last, upstairs. After a few minutes, I heard clomping feet and voices. Flashlight beams
bounced around. "Be careful of her on this turn." "Watch
the railing, it's loose." And "We'll need some signatures before we take her."

Take her? Take her? Take my mother?

I jumped to my feet. Without meaning to, I smashed into
the old coffee table and upset an empty candy dish. It hit the
floor and split into two perfect pieces. I just found Momma.
No one could take her away now.

"My aunt's here to help," I said, rushing forward. "We
can take over now. We can do it . . . together."

Everyone, Aunt Linda included, stood stock-still in the
living room. Momma lay on a stretcher, covered in a blanket
and bound up tight with dark belts that crossed her chest
and stomach and legs.

Only one paramedic glanced my way, then behind him as he let the legs of the stretcher down to the floor.

"Where you going? Where you going with my mother? She can't leave." In a few steps I was by Momma's side. I reached for her, catching her hand in mine.

"Lacey," Aunt Linda said. She came up beside me. "They're taking Angela in for help."

"No," I said. Panic clutched at me. "She doesn't like going out. I'll take care of her. I have. And you're here. You can help now. Like before."

"Lacey." Aunt Linda's breath was warm in my face, smelling of spearmint. "Let her go."

"No." I pushed the words through my teeth. "I can take care of her. It's my job. Even if you don't feel like it."

"Not anymore," someone said, but I almost didn't hear them.

Momma looked at me then. "Baby?" she said. Her voice was slow and soft, just about not there.

"I'm here, Momma." I jerked away from Aunt Linda and leaned close to my mother, so close I could smell sweat, could see her greasy-looking hair, could see her scratches and that blood. I crooned the words at her, like she was the child and I was the mother. "Momma, are you okay now? You want me to tell them to let you loose? I can do a better job this time."

"Baby?" Momma almost couldn't get the words out. She seemed that tired. "I'm right as rain."

A gentle peace filled me like warm water.

"Thank goodness," I said.

Momma would be okay. For a second I thought I might fall to my knees from exhaustion and relief.

"You can visit a minute more," the ambulance lady said. "We need to get her to the hospital. Your mother needs medical attention."

I didn't look at that woman. I pretended like she wasn't even there.

Aunt Linda came up close behind me. A policeman took notes on a tiny pad, using his flashlight like a candle. Another spoke into a radio.

Momma tugged at me with her fingertips. I bent down close to her mouth. "You tell Granddaddy I'll be back," she whispered. "You tell him we'll finish what we started later."

I pulled away from my mother then, like her hand was the sun and had burned me.

"What?"

"You tell him," Momma said. Her voice was light, like she had just a bit of life left in her.

I stumbled back, bumping into Aunt Linda.

No, no, nonono!

Aunt Linda tried to put her arms around me, but I would

191

have none of that. "Too late," I said over my shoulder. "Too late."

The ambulance people started out of the house, Momma with them.

I hurried alongside her, outside into the overgrown darkness. I had to hear that again. It meant something to me. It meant something.

"Momma," I said. "What did you say?"

"You tell him."

"Wait." I jogged now. My feet slapping at the wet earth with a pancake sound. The paramedics wrestled trying to push the stretcher, then decided to carry Momma and tucked the legs of her bed away.

"She doesn't weigh anything," one of them said.

"You gotta get better," I said. "You hear me? You gotta get better."

Momma didn't answer.

"You gotta get better now."

Fear ran down my arms. Different than when I was in the house. I could fight Granddaddy's ghost when I could see him. But I couldn't take on Momma's demons. That scared me more than anything else.

From the porch Aunt Linda called, "Lacey." I ignored her. Instead, I stayed beside Momma, then stood near the back of the ambulance where it opened like a huge, bright mouth and gobbled her up whole.

"You gotta get better now," I said. "You have to, Momma."

"Lacey?" Aunt Linda called after me.

Momma said nothing.

The mist of rain started again. Far away lightning split the sky. After a long moment, thunder rolled up and gave us a tap.

"Tell her good-bye," the ambulance lady said. I saw now her hair was as red as dawn.

"I can't," I said.

"She's going to be okay," the lady said. She touched my shoulder. "We'll take care of her for you. I promise."

"She'll be fine," one of the policemen said.

But I knew in my heart of hearts, that wasn't the truth. And now I had to say good-bye. What if I didn't see her again? "I love you," I said.

She didn't answer.

"I love you, Momma."

They shut the doors then. Got last-minute signatures from Aunt Linda. I watched that ambulance drive away. Some of the neighbors still stood outside. A few wandered away.

For a moment I thought to run after that ambulance.

"Momma, I love you!" I screamed the words, but my voice didn't go far. It got stuck in the wetness and the trees and the dark. I stood out there in the mist that turned to a light rain then quit again. I watched the neighbors go in their homes. Listened to them talk as they went. Heard Aunt Linda call for me, saying that some boy named Aaron was on the phone, then shut the screen door behind her when I didn't answer.

Still I stood outside. Knowing. Knowing Momma wasn't gonna get better.

Not now.

And maybe never?

How could it all end like this?

I flopped down on the ground, soaking myself to the bone. But I didn't care. I watched the place the ambulance went. And I cried.

I thought of Momma and her ghost. I thought of her wanting to kill me. And herself. I thought of the pain that made her want to do such a thing.

Aunt Linda came outside. She brought a housecoat and wrapped it around my shoulders. Then she sat right down next to me.

I kept watching the road. For what? Momma to come back? I didn't know.

My poor momma. My poor, sick momma.

I cried hard then. Aunt Linda pulled me to her and I let her. Let her pet my hair, let my shoulders ease some.

So maybe, I thought after the longest time, maybe Momma wasn't going to be getting any better.

But.

I took in a deep breath. A deep, cleansing breath. I wiped at my face with both hands.

But *I* had to. I had to get better or I might end up like her. I couldn't let my granddaddy boss me around. Couldn't let those thoughts in anymore. Behind me the lights of the house turned on, splashing across the yard, not quite reaching us.

"Lacey." Aunt Linda's voice made me jump. I looked into her face, dark in the night. "You feeling any better, honey? You ready to go in?"

I looked into my aunt's face. Her eyes red, her nose pink, from crying? She was crying, too? For Momma? Or for me? For all three of us?

"I don't want to go inside," I said. My voice sounded like I had a cold, like I had been coughing too long.

Aunt Linda didn't say anything. I stared back across the road, past the orange of the streetlamp, the same direction the ambulance had gone. The same way Momma had gone.

"I'm all alone now," I said, my voice coming out a sad

whisper. "All alone." Saying the words made my heart feel empty.

Aunt Linda rocked me into her.

"No, baby," she said. "No you aren't. I'm here, too."

I'm here, too.

The words were like sweet medicine. Soothing.

"Maybe," I said, whispering, "maybe I am just like her."

Aunt Linda let out a little gasp. "Oh my goodness, Lacey, you are not. No you aren't. You, my sweet girl, you are right as the summer. And strong as an old work horse. No one could have done what you've done."

That was what Aaron had said.

Maybe the two of them were right.

Maybe I was strong.

I would get better, no matter what. Because I did *not* want to be my mother. Not at all.

"Ready?" Aunt Linda said after a while.

I nodded.

Then I went in the house. Determined.

IN MY DREAM, the room is full of books and Mr. Dewey flies straight to me. He perches on my finger and whistles a Disney song.

"I'm back," Aunt Linda says. "I'm back."

"And so's Mr. Dewey," I say.

There is a framed picture of Momma. She's thin and her face is scarred, but she smiles at me when I look at her through the glass.

"You gotta get better, now," Momma says. Her voice sounds just like mine. "You gotta get better, Lacey."

Aunt Linda says, "I'll take care of her, Angela."

"She will," I say. "And I'll take care of me, too."

Even dreaming, this is my choice.